Play Along
(With Me)

Play Along
(With Me)

Bob LaRosa

ISBN: 979-8-218-14503-3

Illustrations: Anna Christiano
Cover Design and Formatting: Susi Clark of Creative Blueprint Design

*To my wife Beth whose patience
and love got me through this.*

Contents

Masters the Kitchen

Cast

N: Narrator

Stephy, Stephanie: House cat able to speak fluently to all non-human characters

Beth: Stephanie's owner, married to Bob

Bob: Stephanie's owner, married to Beth

Radio: Host of *The Magic Rolling Pin* radio show

Fireman: Ordinary fire fighter

~Act 1~

N: Strangely, our story opens in a little house on Bennett Street and not in the great cooking schools of Europe. Our student, Stephanie, does indeed take an interest in the culinary arts—finding there is great delight in rolling out dough. You see, it all started during a beautiful Saturday morning in May as Beth and Bob were leaving to run errands.

Bob: Goodbye, Stephanie.

Beth: Be good, Stephanie!

Stephy: Oh, will those words ever stop haunting me?

N: With great indignation, Stephanie strolls into the front room and up onto the couch for a well-deserved nap. However, something else is occupying space there.

Stephy *(jumping back)***:** What is this? A book on my couch?

N: Upon looking closer…

Stephy: A cookbook? Who could have been so inconsiderate as to leave a—hey! Gee, that looks pretty good.

N: Stephy noses through the directions for tuna casserole.

Stephy: Wow! I never knew reading could be so interesting! Get a load of these pictures!

N: Indeed, mouth-watering recipes with full-color illustrations make the impossible seem easy.

Stephy: You know, I'll bet I could whip up a little something and really surprise Beth and Bob!

N: Quickly, it's off the couch and into the wilds of the kitchen. A kitten must know the territory to succeed!

Stephy: Let's see now, pots, pans, cat food, yep! Everything I need seems to be here. Heck, an apron and stove thrown in too! I'm ready for anything.

N: Ah camera two, a close-up of the before and after disaster shots, please. Now it should be pointed out that nothing is ever really out of reach for a kitten. A flash and she's up on the sink. A mere side swipe and the tap water is flowing beautifully…

Stephy: I'm going to need a little music to maintain the mood.

N: A nearby transistor radio receives a left-rear-paw kick and flips on to the floor.

Radio: OK! And stay tuned for *The Magic Rolling Pin Show*! This week our host will concentrate on pies!

Stephy: Yeah, what could be easier than that?

~Act 2~

N: The magic rolling pin takes her listening audience through the maze of making dough and smashing it onto a pie plate. Stephy finds the floor rising toward the ceiling as one attempt after another does not come out quite right. Finally, Stephy does create the perfect water and dough mix and has long since developed a mean four-footed pie stomp that defies description.

Radio: OK, now the really hard part.

Stephy: Hey, what do you call what we just lived through? I'm running out of dishes here!

Radio: We must now decide what kind of pie filling we will use.

Stephy: What else is there? Where is my bag of cat food?

N: A thorough scan of the kitchen and…

Stephy: OK! Now I'm ready!

Radio: Great! Now you're cooking! Uh, sorry, I always wanted to say that.

Stephy: Oh please, leave the bad jokes to Bob!

Radio: Now spread the filling into the pie evenly, and don't be stingy.

Stephy: Yeah! Go for it! Bonsai cat food!

N: A frenzy of activity ensues, and when the flour dust clears…

Radio: Now we must add some yeast.

Stephy: Right, yeast we forget! (Paw over mouth to suppress giggle.) Oh, I can't believe this is coming out so good. Why haven't I done this before?

N: There's a reason for everything, Stephanie.

Radio: Good! Now we'll need a deft touch for the pie top!

Stephy: A what?

Radio: Roll out the dough again and carefully place it over the top of the pie.

Stephy: Oh, OK!

N: A bountiful blend of cat food, dough, and cat fur is placed on top of the stove and…

Radio: Now set the oven for three hundred fifty degrees and bake.

Stephy: Oh come on now, don't get technical.

N: Stephy had seen Mom cook vegetables on the stove before, and that's just a little step away from baking pies, you know.

Stephy: OK! Burners on! All systems go!

Radio: Let's go to a few hundred commercials, and we'll be back in forty-five minutes.

N: With all the burners blazing away on the stovetop, Stephy retired to the front room to rest up for the next phase.

~ *Act 3* ~

N: It's theorized the fire department arrived only minutes before Beth and Bob. A small kitchen fire was reported by an alert neighbor who heard smoke detectors and saw a rather distraught kitten with a plant spritzer in one paw and marshmallows on a stick in the other. Very, very strange.

Beth: Bob! The fire truck is at our house! Get Stephy out of there!

N: Just then, a fireman raced out carrying a shaking blob of dough, with a tail.

Fireman: Does she belong to you?

Bob: That depends.

Fireman *(handing Stephy to Bob)***:** OK, fire's out! Let's get back to the station!

N: Our trio all head inside to start the clean-up.

Stephy *(eyes closed to become invisible)***:** I wonder if *The Magic Rolling Pin* has days like this.

N: The fire had been contained to the kitchen, and after a couple of hours of work, all was basically back to normal.

Beth: Bob! Come into the front room for a minute!

Bob *(arriving at the door)*: What is it, Beth?

Beth: Look, my cookbook has tiny cat footprints running through every page! You don't suppose…

N: Now no one knows for sure what really happened that day, but be sure you're here next time when Stephy does who knows what to who knows whom!

WELCOME

Unorganized Crime

Cast

N: Narrator

Stephy, Stephanie: House cat able to speak fluently to all non-human characters

Spidey: Delusional spider who enjoys Shakespeare

Bee Quiet: Undisputed crime boss

Rocky Raccoon: Second-in-command, friend of Stephanie

Squirrelly: Unsatisfied, impatient gang member

~*Act 1*~

N: Our story opens in a little house on Bennett Street. Deep into August now, the heat index has climbed from broil to incinerate. Stephanie, sporting her luxurious year-round fur coat, has noticed the weather and says…

Stephy: Hey! I need my backyard air-conditioned at all times! Uncomfortable kitten here, people. EMERGENCY!

N: Stephanie looks around and finds she is alone with the exception of an uninterested spider.

Stephy: Well, what do you think? I suppose you'll say "don't sweat it," right?

Spidey *(to himself)*: Oh, what a tangled web we weave… (Out loud) Yeah, it's hot, but not a lot. We'll cool down quick, if we don't get caught.

Stephy: Huh?

Spidey: Follow me, up this tree, and there you'll see a better bee.

N: Confused, Stephanie follows, climbing behind the delusional spider and finds…

Bee Quiet: Greetings, Spidey! What brings you so far up in the world?

Spidey: A new recruit, strong legs to boot. Name's Stephy.

Bee Quiet: Hi, Stephy, don't mind him. I think he's a Shakespearean throwback or something. What's your story?

Stephy *(glancing over her shoulder toward the house)*: I'm with them.

Bee Quiet: What? No way! You live with fly swatting, bug-spraying humans?! Spidey, you know better than this! GOODBYE!

N: But Bee Quiet does pause long enough to hear…

Stephy: Wait! I can change! Give me a chance here, will ya?

Bee Quiet: OK, one chance. Meet us tonight at sunset by the flower garden and we'll see.

~*Act 2*~

N: The sultry evening rendezvous hour finally arrives, and Stephanie, stepping off her back porch, finds an unexpected mob.

Bee Quiet: OK, guys, this is Stephy! She lives with humans, but she's seen the light and now wants to convert.

Rocky Raccoon: Alright then. If the big bee says you're in, you're in! We've got a hit planned for tonight next door at the Murphy's house. You're the lookout, OK?

Stephy: Ah, sure. Why not?

Rocky Raccoon: Awesome. Stephy, meet Squirrely and Skunkel.

Squirrelly: Enough already. When do we go?

Bee Quiet: We'll keep to the plan. Rocky, you ring the doorbell. When the door opens, Skunkel, do your aromatic splendor trick. While the humans run out, we run in. Ah, Stephy, you watch for the dog.

Stephy: THE DOG?!

Squirrelly: Come on! Those nuts they're storing inside aren't getting any fresher, you know!

N: Like clockwork, a doorbell sounds, a door opens, a skunk runs in, and you can imagine the rest.

Bee Quiet: We're in! Look for the honey jar first!

N: A frenzy of bumbling burglars rampage through the house while outside…

Stephy *(to herself)*: I've seen their dog Brutus before. He's humongous with fangs. Yeah, I'll just scream and run.

N: A sudden crash draws the lookout's attention inside. When she looked back at the yard, a snarling figure stands before her.

~ *Act 3* ~

N: Stephanie's world goes into a temporarily frozen state. Then…

Stephy *(running inside)*: Ahhhhhh!

N: Squirrelly drops his jar of peanuts, Skunkel is out of ammunition, and Bee Quiet is waist-deep in honey. Things are looking bleak.

Rocky Raccoon: Jump up on the table! Dogs can't climb! We'll rush to the exits later as a group!

N: Meanwhile, Stephy has launched herself onto a kitchen counter and somehow knocked an open bag of dog treats onto the floor. Brutus stops, sniffs, and settles in for the unexpected snack.

Spidey *(on the wall over the kitchen door)*: Humans incoming! Every man for himself!

Bee Quiet: I'll buzz the first one through. Spidey, drop a web on the rest. Survivors meet at the picnic table! Break for it now, go, go, go!

N: In the dark, in the chaos, animals rush out chased by dog while humans rush in. Arms, legs, and tails collide at the door with more than a little screaming thrown in. Then a mere eternity later…

Bee Quiet *(at the picnic table)*: We made it! We're all here and in one piece!

Squirrelly: Yeah, with nothing to show for it!

Bee Quiet: Next time, guys. Right now let's lick our wounds and count our lucky stars. We'll meet back at Stephy's place tomorrow.

N: Stephy watches as her friends melt into the warm night. Turning, she sees little Spidey climbing off the picnic table saying…

Spidey: To bee or not to bee…

Asterisk

Cast

N: Narrator

Stephy, Stephanie: House cat able to speak fluently to all non-human characters

Beth: Stephanie's owner, married to Bob

Bob: Stephanie's owner, married to Beth

Question Mark: Disagreeable, bad-tempered character

Asterisk: Friend of Stephanie

Dash: Friend of Stephanie

Semicolon: Friend of Stephanie

Exclamation Mark: Friend of Stephanie, Question Mark's big brother

~Act 1~

N:　　　Our story begins in a little house on Bennett Street. On a beautiful fall evening just as the house was getting quiet, Stephanie enters the den and jumps to the top of a bookcase. Unfortunately, carelessly placed books are waiting for her up there.

Stephy:　　Oh no! Who put these obstructions on top of my bookcase? I'm losing my balance, I'm heading south!

N:　　　Stephanie and half a dozen books go over the side, but instead of landing on a book, she lands in one.

Stephy:　　Where am I? What happened to the den? What is this place?

N:　　　Nothing but silence came to her ears and of course curiosity carried her into the story line. Carefully looking around, she spotted…

Asterisk:　Welcome to the literary world, outsider. Care to move deeper into the plot?

Stephy:　　Who are you? You kind of look like a tiny splotch to me.

Asterisk:　Hey! I'll have you know I'm an integral part of the punctuation group. If you care to, I can introduce you to others, we're used in writing to separate sentences and clarify their meaning.

Stephy:　　Sure, why not. I'm kind of lost here. A little clarification would be most helpful. What are their names?

Asterisk:　Well I just saw a few before you came in. Comma, semicolon, and dash should be on the next page. Follow me.

Stephy:　　How many are there in the club?

Asterisk:　Oh, there are fourteen in all. I doubt if we'll see all of them though. Some are rather obscure, you know how it is.

N: Stephanie follows close behind, not daring to fall off the page by leaping too far ahead in the story.

Asterisk: Here we are, um, Question Mark, got a minute?

Question Mark: Questions, questions, everybody's got questions! I need a vacation. Oh, who do we have here?

Asterisk: Stephy, meet Question Mark. Question Mark, behave yourself.

Stephy: Hi, I'm just passing through. Do you know where the last page is? I'm in need of dinner and a nap in the real world.

Question Mark: Another question? You're just like the rest! Yeah, last page is over by the back cover. I'm needed on page thirty. Come on, it's on the way.

~Act 2~

N: On her way to page thirty, Stephanie had the opportunity to meet both Semicolon and Dash. Both were far more amiable than Question Mark appeared to be. At one point Stephanie wanted to know what the huge paper bookmark was all about, but she was afraid to ask another question.

Asterisk: We wanted you to see how beautifully structured the sentences around here are, Stephy. Mind if we step into the margin for a moment?

Question Mark: Knock off the questions, Asterisk, you're giving the kitten the wrong idea. Statements everyone! Stay with the statements!

Dash: Don't mind him, Stephy, he woke up on the wrong side of the title page this morning. From the margins you can see clear to the number on the bottom down there. See? Quit grumbling, Question Mark, some questions are necessary, you know.

Semicolon: Hey, mind if I tag along? Can't wait to introduce you to our Greek hero, Parentheses. He usually brackets off Question Mark quite nicely.

Asterisk: We wanted to know if you had a clue what that sudden jarring crash was this morning, Stephy. We all felt it. I think we've got a couple crumpled and torn pages because of the event.

Stephy *(thinking quickly)***:** Yeah? Probably Bob stumbling about. He's not much for balance, you know. How do you repair things like that around here?

Semicolon: Exclamation Mark! He's Question Mark's big brother. We usually ask him!

Asterisk: Right! Sometimes books are so damaged though, and they end up being thrown away. Best we settle for what we can get like being donated or traded in. Beats going to the incinerator, I think!

Stephy: Incinerator! For a crumpled or torn page? Maybe between Exclamation Mark and myself we can avoid that! Where is he anyway?

Dash: Closer than you think. Turn the page.

N: Stephanie could always adapt to any situation as it arrived, but nothing could have prepared her for Exclamation Mark.

Exclamation Mark: HI, OUTSIDERS ARE ALWAYS WELCOMED HERE!

Stephy: Is he always this loud?

Question Mark: You were warned about excessive questions, Stephy. Do you want to get to the last page or what?

~ *Act 3* ~

N: Stephanie wanted to repair the damage done to the book and be on her way home before dark. Turning to Semicolon, she requests an inspection and is directed to page fifty-two.

Stephy: Semicolon, would you and Exclamation Mark hold the page taut while I jump and stomp it flat? We'll have Asterisk roll all over its surface when I'm done.

N: Working together, they flattened the wrinkled page into a permanently level surface, sufficient for reading. No amount of stressful manipulating would repair the tear however, and Stephanie realized she would need outside help.

Stephy: Alright, gang, our next step is to hold as many pages up in this open book in hopes the den's fan will rattle the paper.

Semicolon: What good would that do?

Stephy: The owner might hear the noise and glue the torn page, making the book like new again.

Asterisk: Even all of us working in unison can't do that. We'll need the printed words' help to lift that many pages simultaneously.

Exclamation Mark: NO PROBLEM! WORDS, ASSEMBLE AND LIFT ON THREE! NOW ONE, TWO, THREE, LIFT!

N: Beth came into the den upon hearing the fluttering sound of paper. Picking up the books, she noticed one had a torn page and carried it to a nearby table for repair.

Asterisk: God job, all! Now reassemble into your original position and hope we don't misspell anything.

Beth *(putting the book on the table)*: That's funny, there are tiny noises coming from this book! I'll just get the glue.

Asterisk: Stephy, help! Your giant dropped a corner of the torn page I'm on. I'll be on the floor in a second, she'll probably step on me!

Stephy: I hear you, good buddy! Be there in a jiffy!

N: Beth re-enters the room and imagines she sees Stephanie trying to stuff a page's torn corner into the book.

Beth: Stephy, get down from the table! What were you doing up there anyway?

Stephy *(to herself)*: You wouldn't believe me, Mom. You just wouldn't believe me.

Stephanie, Queen of Sheba

Cast

N: Narrator

Stephy, Stephanie: House cat able to speak fluently to all non-human characters

Beth: Stephanie's owner, married to Bob

Bob: Stephanie's owner, married to Beth

Court Jester, Chief Chef, Fritina: All members of the royal court

General Pete Sake, General Why Not: Head of military personnel

Devon: King of neighboring country

Messenger: Lowly individual both meek and mild

~*Act 1*~

Beth and Bob: Stephy, we're home!

Stephanie *(to herself)*: What was my first clue?

Bob: Have you been as good as you could be?

Stephanie *(to herself)*: No, I was better than I meant to be.

Beth: Bob, Stephy looks a little down. Why don't you cheer her up while I make supper?

Bob: OK, come on, Stephy. Let's get dinner for you and then we'll play Kill Catnip Mousey!

Stephanie: Yeah, OK! Now you're talking! You know it gets lonely when they're away. I really need somebody to wait on me full time.

N: After dinner, Beth holds Stephanie and brushes her luxurious fur coat.

Stephanie: Ahhhh! That's it! Oh, a little to the left please.

Bob: Man, that cat's really got it made! When you think of how many people refer to pets as dumb animals—wow! I mean what's so dumb in sending the two of us off to work every day while she does a little languishing at home? Her royal lifestyle is truly that of the Queen of Sheba!

Stephanie: Hey, I like that! Yeah, it fits! My subjects, await my commands!

N: Suddenly Stephanie stretches, signaling to Beth that brush time is over.

Stephanie: I think I'll nap now. You may conduct your lives in a quiet, orderly fashion.

~Act 2~

N: While she sleeps, Stephanie is dreaming of her catdom with its many adoring citizens and tons of cat food. It would appear she could get used to all this very easily.

Stephanie *(dreaming)*: You there, what do you do?

Court Jester: Oh Queen Stephy, I'm your castle clown. I'll entertain you royally.

Stephanie: You may proceed!

N: While the entertainment committee is standing on his head and juggling with his feet, another subordinate approaches the throne.

Stephanie: Yes, and who might you be?

Chief Chef: I, madame, am head of your kitchens. I would serve you dinner and await your selection of menu.

Stephanie: Back to you in a minute. Don't go away. Ah, you there! Yes, you in the back! Come forward and greet your queen.

N: From the back of the great hall advances a stunning example of proper dress and behavior.

Fritina: Your Highness, I've been appointed your personal adviser on manners and good grooming. After all, appearances are important.

Stephanie: OK, guards, march her off to the dungeon.

N: With a wave of her paw, Fritina is gone, and the chef is back.

Stephanie: Um, tuna please with a dash of rosemary on the side.

Chief Chef: Very good, your Kittenship!

N: A blare of trumpets heralds in another set of problems.

Stephanie: Now what? Aren't there any coffee breaks around here?

N: A messenger from a nearby kingdom approaches the throne.

Messenger: Stephanie, Queen Of Sheba, this is to announce the declaration of war on you and your catdom by Devon, King of Dogs! Please don't kill me and have a nice day.

Stephanie: Of course. In town five minutes and someone declares war on you. Send him home with a doggy bone for his king.

~ *Act 3* ~

N: The midnight oil burns while Stephy confers with her generals. It seems she could have dreamed up a stronger country.

General Pete Sake: And as I see it, that's the only way we will win, Your Highness.

Stephanie: Should we do that, we will forfeit our catnip fields! Never! What do you say, General Why Not?

General Why Not: I agree the fields are important, but there's no other solution to the problem, oh Great One. Most significant is the fact that we need more time to gather troop strength.

Stephanie: Hmmm. Thank you, that will be all. I have a better idea. Bring Fritina here right away!

N: While the Queen waits, her eyes flash and her tail swishes as the idea solidifies in her brain.

Fritina: You sent for me, my Queen?

Stephanie: Yes, we need to avert a war and you are going to help me do it.

N: Stephanie explains the plan to Fritina and soon both agree on how to get out of this mess.

Stephanie: I want you to ride in with me and teach me a little dignity as well.

Fritina: Oh gladly, and I think it may just work too.

N: Upon Stephanie's orders, the generals have their troops ready to march, though each is carrying a sack instead of a gun. Hours later, under the cover of night, Stephanie's army has surrounded the enemy. Stephanie then orders the burning of the sacks. Very soon, all the dog soldiers of King Devon's army are running around acting like puppies again. Stephanie sends a messenger to bring King Devon to her and the two finally speak!

Stephanie: You we're going to attack me?

Devon (dazed): Well yeah. At least it seemed a good idea at the time. I can see now it wasn't. How about calling the whole thing off?

Stephanie: Fine.

Devon: What kind of terrible gas did you use on us anyway?

Stephanie: Catnip! And we'll use it again if necessary!

Devon: No need, I can see we're no match for you.

N: Stephanie accepts the sword of surrender from Devon and the war is over. On the return trip home, she again speaks to Fritina.

Stephanie: Wow, Fritina, this queen stuff is a lot of hard work! I figured it was just a be-waited-on-and-get-paid-for-it job.

Fritina: No, my Queen. It's a life of decision-making and awesome responsibility.

Stephanie: Well look, kid, it's time I woke up, so I'm leaving you in charge. Rule good and I'll be back in a few dreams.

N: With that, our favorite feline opens her eyes and sees the spare bedroom on Bennett Street again. Stretching, she heads for her food dish and ponders.

Stephanie: It's great to be back. I mean, it's lonely at the top. Really, who could I be better than me? Oh well. Hey! My food dish is empty! Who's in charge here anyway?

Dwarf Shortage

Cast

N: Narrator

Stephy, Stephanie: House cat able to speak fluently to all non-human characters

Beth: Stephanie's owner, married to Bob

Bob: Stephanie's owner, married to Beth

Danny Boy: Leprechaun

~*Act 1*~

N: Our story opens on a little road near Bennett Street. Stephanie's back-yard privileges have quickly expanded due to her "what they don't know won't hurt me" policy. Subsequently, the call of the open road could not be ignored!

Stephy: Who are you?

Danny Boy: I'm a little person, a leprechaun if you like. You can call me Danny Boy!

Stephy: OK, whatcha doing?

Danny Boy: Making tiny shoes! You see, I'm a cobbler. Looks like you could use some! Maybe a double pair in a size zero?

Stephy: Sure! I've never had any, could you color coordinate with my collar?

N: Stephanie looks around but doesn't see a workbench.

Danny Boy: Coming right up! That will be two pieces of gold please.

Stephy: Oh, I'm a little short, how about a trade instead?

Danny Boy: Depends on if you can refrain from the diminutive references and give me housing instead.

Stephy: You've got it! Let's go!

N: The two friends quickly find themselves on Bennett Street as Danny Boy explains…

Danny Boy: You see, there once was a factory employing dozens of wee people like myself. Everything was great until the flood. Since then, we've all gone our own way.

Stephy: You mean that rainstorm we got last week? That was just a shower! Don't worry, we'll set you up with everything you need. And hey, Beth and Bob don't need to know about it either!

~Act 2~

N: Stephanie sets Danny Boy up with deluxe under-the-bookcase accommodations and helps him secure scraps of materials from all over the house. Soon, a tiny workshop is pumping out shoes and a mischievous little person is "borrowing" other items to be sold for gold as well.

Beth: Have you seen my lipstick? It was right on top of the nightstand last night! And what's with the four-leaf clover? Is this some kind of joke?

Bob: Nope, but I received a clover as well. It was left on top of the dresser where my watch used to be. Let's have a little talk with you-know-who.

N: An angry Stephanie placed in an unjustified time out is planning a little conference of her own. Meanwhile a rather unrepentant Danny Boy is just getting his crime spree underway.

Bob: I'm seeing a flash from the corner of my eye! Are you picking up on that strong shamrock scent too?

Beth: Yes, and with St. Patrick's day coming tomorrow, I think I'm sensing a pattern here. Isn't that a shillelagh by the door? And who ever heard of a rainbow inside of a house? There's a joker loose from the deck!

Danny Boy: They're onto me! I'll need help! Sure and begorrah, I've got to get that shillelagh back. Where's Stephanie when I need her?

N: Her time out over, Stephanie tracks the elf with her heightened sense of sight and smell. In no time, she has the leprechaun cornered and begging for mercy.

Stephy: Put it all back! I'm not taking the fall for this!

Danny Boy: OK! Let's hang together or we'll hang separately! Get the shillelagh from the she-giant and we'll get this over with right now!

~ *Act 3* ~

N: Beth has hidden the magic stick in the cupboard and dragged out the vacuum cleaner. With Bob's help, she has moved the furniture to the center of the room and is pursuing a devilishly quick miniature phantom. Without the shillelagh, the poor leprechaun can't disappear and is tiring fast. Shaking with fear, Danny Boy finds himself trapped in a corner with the vacuum only inches away.

Beth: Now I've got you!

Danny Boy: A deal, lass, let's make a deal!

Beth: I'm listening, make it quick!

Danny Boy: I'll return it all, just let me go! And for your trouble I'll throw in a wish as well. What do you say?

Bob: Watch out, he's a trickster! We'll need something of his to seal the deal.

N: At just that moment, Stephanie enters the room carrying the shillelagh in her mouth. Bob grabs the kitten and its contents in one swift movement and the negotiations begin.

Beth: We know your tricks. First return our things, then we'll talk.

Bob: Stephy, when I say *bite*, CRUSH THAT SHILLELAGH!

N: Within an instant, all the stolen items are laying at Beth's feet. With a sly look on his face, the elf looks up, grabs his shillelagh from Stephanie's jaws, and says…

Danny Boy: And your wish, lass?

Beth: I wish everyone has a nice St. Patrick's Day!

Danny Boy *(striking the floor with his stick)*: DONE!

N: And he was gone.

Justice for All

Cast

N: Narrator

Stephy, Stephanie: House cat able to speak fluently to all non-human characters

Tumble Weed: Deputy, friend of Stephanie

Deputy Dan: Deputy, friend of Stephanie

Bank Teller: Bank employee

Bad Bart: Notorious outlaw

~Act 1~

N: Our story opens in a little house on Bennett Street. On a lazy summer afternoon, Stephanie is camped out in the living room in front of the TV when sleep finally overcomes her.

Stephy *(mumbling sleepily)*: What kind of western was that? The sheriff didn't get the bad guy, the horses all ran away, and there wasn't a single cat in the entire show! Why, if I was there…

N: Between the warm splash of sunlight she was in on the carpet, and the fact she was out all night, her eyes gently closed. Sleepily, she envisions a time when justice was scarce on the old frontier.

Tumble Weed: Sheriff Stephy! Come quick! There's a shootout at the OK Corral!

Stephy: Can't it wait? I'm in the middle of lunch here, deputy.

Tumble Weed: There's also a brawl at the saloon.

Stephy: Anything else?

Tumble Weed: Just an illegal cattle drive stampeding down Main Street.

N: The sheriff drops her tuna fish sandwich, drinks a last gulp of water, and goes out into the street.

Stephy: I'll take the shootout, you take the brawl. We'll meet up on Main Street in fifteen minutes! Any questions?

Tumble Weed: Can I take Splinter with me?

Stephy: Sure, just be certain he's back in his pen when you're done.

N: Stephanie strolls over to the corral while Tumble Weed unleashed the nine-hundred-pound grizzly.

~Act 2~

N: Sheriff Stephanie arrives roughly when the gun battle is ending. She leans up against a hitching post, yawns, and says to no one in particular…

Stephy: Whoever's alive at the end of this, come with me. If you hurry, there's probably still hot coffee back at the jail. District judge's not due in till next week.

N: Deputy Tumble Weed is having a harder time of it. Splinter broke loose two blocks from the bar and scared all the horses out of town. Meanwhile, Bad Bart and his outlaw gang is robbing the stagecoach out on the trail when he notices a heard of saddled horses go by. Things really went downhill though when someone ate the Sheriff's sandwich.

Deputy Dan: Sheriff! Tumble Weed lost Splinter!

Stephy *(arriving at the jail house)*: OK! Lock these two up and meet me at the bar brawl.

Deputy Dan: Ah, there's one other thing.

Stephy: The cattle parade down Main Street?

Deputy Dan: Naw, Bad Bart just held up the stage. Word is he's headed for the bank in town. Where are the horses?

Stephy: It's just one of those days, Dan. Hey! Where's my sandwich?

Tumble Weed: Sheriff! I'm glad I caught you in time. We've got trouble!

Stephy: You're not kidding! Someone ate my sandwich!

Tumble Weed: OK, there's that. I was referring to something else though.

Stephy: Let me guess. The brawl? The cattle drive? The stagecoach disaster? I took care of the shootout. What did I miss?

Tumble Weed: The fire!

N: Stephanie looks out the window and sees the hotel across the street going up in flames.

~ *Act 3* ~

Stephy: Tumble Weed! Get up on the roof and ring that fire bell! Deputy Dan, help them push the fire wagon to the hotel! You two in jail, you're deputized! Go break up that bar fight!

Deputy Dan and Tumble Weed: What will you do?

Stephy: Thought I'd hang out at the bank.

N: On a better day, Stephanie would have ridden her horse to the bank. As things are, however, she gets to see firsthand how much damage the cattle stampede has caused. Uppermost in her mind though is catching the sandwich thief.

Bank Teller: Morning, Sheriff! How's your day going?

Stephy: Nothing unusual. Mind if I hang out in the side lobby?

N: Just then, Bad Bart and company ride in. Expecting no trouble getting away, they saunter into the bank with pistols drawn.

Bad Bart: Hands up! Put the money in the saddle bag! What's with the fire?

N: At that point, Stephy enters from the lobby with Tumble Weed behind her. Deputy Dan has circled around to the back door.

Stephy: Your turn to reach, Bad Bart! Drop the saddle bags and march this way, all of you!

N: Bad Bart fires but misses! His gang all rush to the door but stop dead in their tracks when they see Splinter. Looking past the grizzly, they can see their horses running off. Guns, money, and pride hit the floorboards. Everybody quietly looks to the sheriff.

Stephy: OK, everyone, before jail, there's a little chore you can help with. How are you at putting out fires? (Stephy mumbling sleepily): At least I caught the bad guys!

Some Assembly Required

Cast

N: Narrator

Stephy, Stephanie: House cat able to speak fluently to all non-human characters

Bob: Stephanie's owner, married to Beth

Flake: Snowman

Doe-a-Deer: Friend of Stephanie

~*Act 1*~

N: On any cold winter evening, Stephanie would normally be found snuggled deep in her blanketed box. On this one particular wintery night however...

Stephy: What was that? There it is again!

N: A graceful leap to the window reveals a speck of light shimmering just above the rapidly deepening backyard snow. Bob, fresh from shoveling the driveway, opens the back door and jumps back screaming...

Bob: Yikes! Where do you think you're going? Stephy, get back here! Does that cat have fur on the brain or what?

Stephy: Worth it! I love to see them jump! Now where did that shimmer go to?

N: A distant disembodied voice responds...

Flake: See that snowball the kids threw into the yard?

Stephy: Yeah, what about it?

Flake: Roll it over to the tree please.

Stephy: Of all the... That would be work! Show yourself first!

N: A bright flash of light below the lowest tree branch is the only response. Stephanie did roll the snowball across the yard as instructed, finding it harder as the ball grew larger and larger.

Stephy *(puffing)*: There! I did it, now what?

Flake: See that second snowball across the way?

Stephy: Yeah? What, you want me to do this again?

Flake: You help me and I'll help you.

N: After a second then, a third snowball was rolled to the tree…

Flake: OK, now the hard part.

Stephy: Are you nuts? I'm exhausted here. What are you anyway?

Flake: I'm the Spirit of Winter! You may call me Flake.

Stephy: Flake sounds about right. What do I do with these things?

Flake: Stack! You know, one on top of the other.

Stephy: Going to need some help here, Flake. Mind if I get Bob?

Flake: Humans? No way! Hire out if you have to. I'll make it worth your while.

N: Stephanie was not one for elaborate planning. She simply looked over her shoulder and saw her friend Doe-a-Deer grazing on shrubs nearby.

Stephy: Hey, Doe-a-Deer, over here! I've got a job for us both!

Flake: Teamwork, I like it! OK, guys, start stacking!

Doe-a-Deer: Where's that voice coming from? Why are we doing this?

Stephy: Go with it, friend! This guy's got deep pockets. We're practically on Easy Street now!

~ Act 2 ~

N: Soon three balls of snow, two rock eyes, and a couple of branch arms were assembled in a humanlike arrangement, creating one fine-looking snowman. The flash of light glowed behind the eyes and then…

Flake *(muffled voice)***:** Hey, I'm back! Ah, a few more rocks for a mouth would help wonders, if you please.

N: With that done, the Stephy-Doe-a-Deer construction crew stepped back to admire their creation.

Doe-a-Deer: Um, I think its pay day.

Flake: Right you are!

N: Flake gathered some snow and rocketed a snowball at pine cones high in the tree. Soon, half the crew was munching happily on the tasty treat.

Stephy: Ahem, forgetting something?

N: A smile crossed Flake's rocky lips as he reached into his pocket and pulled out a big wad of catnip.

Stephy: Now you're talking! Hey, did you hear that?

N: With no actual ears, Flake couldn't hear well enough to pick up on the soft low growls across the yard. He did however see Doe-a-Deer slip quietly behind him and followed Stephy's worried gaze to the coyotes closing in. Almost in a single move, he gathered his friends up in his massive arms and slid on his base down the hill and out of the yard. Within seconds, they were on the street and finally coasted to a stop in the Lowell Field playground.

Flake: Kids! Humans! Sorry, guys, this is where the ride ends!

N: Simultaneously, the passengers were unceremoniously dropped to the ground. Looking up, a confused Stephanie saw a frozen statue of snow where her friend once stood. Then the children spotted the kitten-deer combo and gave chase.

Stephy: Quick! This way! Follow me!

Doe-a-Deer: No, you hop on my back and steer. It'll be quicker. We'll out-distance them in no time, you'll see.

N: Like an old western movie, the two galloped away, much to the amazement of several mothers in the park.

~ *Act 3* ~

N: Several streets over, Doe-a-Deer slowed to a standstill, allowing Stephy to jump off. Looking around, the kitten observed…

Stephy: We're alone, no kids, no coyotes, nothing. We should be happy, but I'm feeling we've got to go back. How about you?

Doe-a-deer: Yeah, those kids could tear him apart. Why do you suppose he froze up like that?

Stephy: Who knows? I live with humans, you know. Mine are weird but harmless. It's the smaller ones you have to be wary of. Let's get back there now!

N: Much to their relief, the playground was deserted by the time they arrived. Flake, however, lay in ruins. Stephanie looked up and saw the now familiar twinkling of light and said…

Stephy: Falling apart are we? Can we give you a hand?

Flake: Very funny. Start rolling some snowballs please.

N: Soon Flake was his old self with a few minor improvements.

Doe-a-Deer: You're looking better than ever, Flake! Love the new add-ons, don't you?

N: Looking down at himself, Flake could see an additional array of snow skis on his feet and a bag full of snowballs at his side.

Flake: Yeah, could have used this earlier during the onslaught.

N: Just then, the skies opened up with a rain snow and ice mix!

Flake: Lovely weather, huh, guys?

N: The two with a heartbeat looked at each other and frowned when suddenly… FOUR COYOTES.!

Stephy: Nowhere to run! Nowhere to hide! You can't throw enough snowballs in time, Flake! Doe-a-Deer, sorry to get you mixed up in this.

Flake: We're not done yet, guys. Stay together and don't move!

N: The ski-shod snowman proceeded to travel ever faster in wide but tightening circles around the coyotes. Soon a tornado effect materialized, sweeping everything up in its path. Then, nothing but warm rain falling on cold snow. Through the resulting fog, both Stephanie and friend searched for the snowman, but to no avail.

Stephy: Come on, Doe-a-Deer, let's get back to Bennett Street. I need to warm up and nap a lot. He'll be back again someday.

Wizard of Bennett Street

Cast

N: Narrator

Stephy, Stephanie: House cat able to speak fluently to all non-human characters

Beth: Stephanie's owner, married to Bob

Bob: Stephanie's owner, married to Beth

Merlin: Ancient magician

Hephaestus: Ancient god of fire and ice

~Act 1~

N: It all begins on a wild, stormy night on Bennett Street. Summer has brought hot, sticky conditions to the area only to be abruptly cooled by a capricious cold front with an accompanying display of thunder and lightning.

Stephy: What's with the racket? I'm trying to sleep here!

N: One graceful leap to the window later...

Stephy: Wow! Daylight in the middle of the night! What will they think of next?

N: Within the lightning flash, Stephanie's keen eyes catches the outline of a figure, hands raised and chanting an incoherent summons.

Stephy: I know that guy wasn't there when I came in. Time for the world's greatest guard cat to do her thing!

N: An open window is quickly found and the startled intruder is soon looking down at a hissing Stephanie.

Merlin: Hello, what's this?

Stephy: You're the one with the explaining to do—ah, how is it that you're able to speak fluent cat?

Merlin: Where I'm from, language is an art, not a barrier. Am I trespassing here? I could teleport out if you like.

Stephy: Well, no. I mean not yet anyway. Who were you summoning?

Merlin: Zeus. He's been a real problem for my monarch. He's a nasty one with his lightning, thunder, and whatnot. No regard for others, you know. We told him: rain, yes, don't bother with the flash and noise. My name is Merlin and yours?

Stephy: Stephy! Who's your king? And where's this Zeus guy from?

Merlin: Why, King Arthur of course. And Zeus? Mount Olympus.

Stephy: Never heard of any of you.

~Act 2~

N: The two friends agreed to meet at Lowell Field later that morning. Stephanie was curious about King Arthur's round table and wanted to know if the chairs were circular as well.

Stephy: Any luck reaching Zeus last night?

Merlin: Nope. Got a hold of his son Hephaestus though. He should be here shortly.

Stephy: What does he do? I'm afraid to ask.

Merlin: Oh you know, god of fire and ice. A more reasonable chap really. He makes weapons for everyone up there in his forge and all. Thought he might get a message to his dad for me.

Stephy: Forge? That sounds old school. How old are your friends?

Merlin: Oh about a thousand centuries or so. Why do you ask?

N: But before Stephanie could reply…

Hephaestus: Who summoned me?

Merlin: I did. Meet Stephanie.

Hephaestus: Hello, creature of the forest. What a strange time you've chosen to live in. How can I serve you, wizard?

Stephy: Wizard? You mean like magician?

Merlin: Afraid so, Stephy. Ah, Hephaestus, would you be so kind as to inform your father his noise bothers future generations of humans as well as King Arthur's subjects? Go ahead, tell him, Stephy!

Stephy: Yeah, that's right. Woke me up last night, you know. And I didn't choose this time to live in, it just sort of worked out that way.

Hephaestus: Tedious Merlin! Dad's not going to change. I've told you this before! In fact before I left, he gave me a message for you.

Merlin: Which is?

N: Hephaestus turned full circle and all of Lowell Field was ablaze.

~ Act 3 ~

N: Fire apparatuses from four neighboring communities arrive within minutes. All were at a loss as to how the fire was started. Meanwhile, background thunder can be heard on a clear, sunny afternoon. After that, things begin to unravel in a most mysterious way.

Merlin: Stephy, I told you Zeus was a nasty one. Sorry about your neighborhood playground. I'm afraid this is just the beginning though.

Stephy: Beginning? And how did we get home so fast?

Bob: Stephy! We were worried about you! Come inside before anything else happens!

Stephy: Let me guess. He can't see you, can he?

Merlin: Nope. I'll need your help out here shortly, little one. Can you see your way out and meet me by the mighty oak behind your home?

Stephy: Can a duck quack? Of course, you're not the only magician around here, you know.

N: Moments later, Stephy is once again outside and ready to assist.

Merlin: Hephaestus would not have come alone! Your world has not evolved to the point where Mount Olympus can be defeated. Even I may not have power enough to protect humankind.

Stephy: If you were trying to get my attention, you've got it! What's the plan?

Merlin: First, I'm going to bestow upon you powers enough to make you a worthy assistant. Then in tandem we will defeat Olympus!

N: Beth and Bob have been glued to their windows since the fire erupted. Now looking out the back window, Beth screams…

Beth: Bob! Stephy is caught in a whirlwind outside! Some kind of shadow figure is standing beside her! Get out there quick!

N: Bob never had a chance to reach Stephy. A flash is all he sees, and when his eyes adjust…

Bob: She's gone!

N: Meanwhile, back at Lowell Field, Stephy and Merlin reappear.

Stephy: OK, you've got to tell me how you do that!

Merlin: No time! Look, standing beside Hephaestus, it's Ares the god of war!

Stephy: OK, now you're scaring me. What do we do?

Merlin: A tactical maneuver, Stephy! Quickly move to your right while I divert their attention. When I yell *Angstrom*, we smite!

Stephy *(moving quickly)*: We what?

N: All further instructions are sent to Stephy telepathically.

Merlin: Stephy, hold both paws up in the air. Concentrate your power on the two gods before you. Together on signal, we will strike a mighty blow.

Stephy: Got you, wizard, ready when you are.

Merlin: Gods of Olympus, back to your own time! Be gone! Angstrom!

N: Weather experts from around the globe were focused on a single point in North America. A weather anomaly never before seen was unfolding at Lowell Field. Called a tornado-earthquake by some, this event featured lightning strikes, rain, wind, ice, and something similar to a fault-line failure, all within a very localized area. Meanwhile, Beth and Bob were watching the news when…

Beth: Bob, look!

N: Stephanie materialized, dematerialized, then finally rematerialized in the living room—right before their eyes. Simultaneously, they looked at one another and said…

Beth and Bob: We don't want to know!

Couch Surfer

Cast

N: Narrator

Stephy, Stephanie: House cat able to speak fluently to all non-human characters

Beth: Stephanie's owner, married to Bob

Bob: Stephanie's owner, married to Beth

Marie: Beth's sister and honorary cat sitter

~Act 1~

N: Our story opens in a little house on Bennett Street. Beautiful June weather has brought early vacation plans to everyone's mind. Stephanie listens in as they discuss their future in detail.

Beth: I love looking at these vacation packages! Check out this train-plane trip to the Rockies! It's full of hotels, meals, and guided tours! We'll have a ball!

Bob: Sounds great, let's make the reservations!

Beth: The trip is only two weeks away. What are we going to do with Stephy?

Bob: Our families have offered accommodations before, let's try our luck there.

Beth: Yes, that would be much better than a kennel. But two weeks with Stephy would be a lot to ask. Better to divide the time among a few households.

Stephanie: Did I hear right? Are they actually thinking of shipping me off somewhere? Won't they miss me to the point of despondency? They'll never make it without me, you know.

N: While not exactly on the same page, our group presses on and preparations are put into play. The trip would afford time to recharge for the adults and a chance to rearrange lives for Stephanie.

~Act 2~

Beth: Everyone has been called, and believe it or not, they said yes!

Bob: Do they understand it is STEPHANIE we're talking about?

Beth: Yep, and better yet, they said don't rush back!

Bob: I hope you told them to call the next one in line if things got out of hand.

N: Beth's instructions to each of her sisters are to take turns caring for Stephanie and call if an emergency arises. The day of departure is quickly upon them, and Stephanie along with a ton of luggage is loaded into the car.

Bob: We're set to go! There's enough food and cat toys packed to keep a hundred cats happy for life.

Beth: I've got the emergency numbers in my purse just in case.

Bob: They don't include ours, do they?

N: Bob receives his well-deserved look of scorn, and they are off to sister Janet's house. Stephanie is confined within her cat carrier and yowls the whole way. A half hour later, the car comes to a stop in front of a large colonial home as we hear…

Beth: She's had all her shots. She knows how to use her box. We really appreciate the help, Janet!

Bob: She has been known to be good on occasion.

N: An hour later on the tarmac, Beth is having second thoughts.

Beth: Maybe we should have brought her along.

Bob: Your cat-loving sisters can handle it. Don't think about it. We'll find a way to repay them somehow.

~ *Act 3* ~

N: Four days into their vacation, a phone message is waiting at the hotel's front desk. Stephanie has been moved to sister Susan's house. The note mentions something about a missing goldfish.

Bob: One cat sitter down, two to go!

Beth: I wonder if I included the kennel's phone number?

N: That might have been prudent, for on day eight, they receive an urgent text message. It reads in part, "Stephanie might enjoy a change of scenery." It seems the litter box and cat never got together. Next up was sister Marie who had two cats of her own.

Bob: Marie can handle anything! Let's go skiing!

Beth: I want my sisters to talk to me again someday.

N: Beth needn't have worried as no more communication arrives until day thirteen. This time an email reads, "Hope you're having a good time. All is well here with one exception. Please call me at nine tonight your time."

Beth: What happened now? Should we go back a day early?

Bob: Why don't we just call and face the music.

N: At the prescribed hour, Beth calls to find a laughing sister Marie at the other end of the line.

Marie: You're not going to believe what happened.

Beth: Try me.

Marie: Well, I was out grocery shopping, and when I got home, instead of the usual kitten tsunami, I was greeted by my neighbor June.

Beth: Oh no, were the police involved?

Marie: Nope. Nothing like that. She did inform me though of a house party of sorts while I was away. She said the mailman heard running and crashing sounds inside my house and asked if she would check it out. When June got there, she saw three kittens in the window with a crumpled lampshade beneath their paws.

Beth: Oh no, what do I owe you?

Marie: Nothing! When I got inside, I saw a dead mouse on the floor and three very proud kittens circling my feet. I had suspected a field mouse had gotten in, but because my kittens are chickens, I was going to call an exterminator. Stephanie saved me a ton of money and taught the others a valuable lesson. Stay out there as long as you like! Stephanie is welcome here anytime!

It's About Time

Cast

N: Narrator

Stephy, Stephanie: House cat able to speak fluently to all non-human characters

Beth: Stephanie's owner, married to Bob

Bob: Stephanie's owner, married to Beth

Eternity: Father Time

Owl Face: Friend of Stephanie

~ Act 1 ~

N: Our story opens just outside a little house on Bennett Street. Lost in thought, a kitten proceeds up the deck stairway and is about to turn left when…

Stephanie: What's this? An old hourglass floating in midair? Have I been out in the sun too long?

N: The apparition glows for a moment then disappears, only to reappear immediately in the hands of an older gentleman.

Stephanie: Enough already! Who are you?

Eternity: Me? I've many names. In ancient Greece, I was called Chronos. Strangely though, none have actually seen me until now. You may call me Eternity.

Stephanie: Yeah? Well I see you just fine. Why the visit? And what's with the vanishing act?

Eternity: I've always been here. In fact, I've always been everywhere at once.

Stephanie: Look, it's hot out here. Come on in and cool off. I'll take the window route and open that locked door from the inside for you.

Eternity: No need, I'm there as well.

N: An extremely confused Stephanie gains access to the living room only to find her new friend sitting comfortably on the couch.

Stephanie: OK, let's try this again. You're Eternity from Ancient Greece. You have a floating hourglass and a magic act like I've never seen. Care to explain?

Eternity: Sure, yesterday, today, and tomorrow are all the same to me. How about you? How does a kitten even know about time? Most try to keep track of me, but none have ever conversed with myself. At least not in this realm. How is this possible you can?

N: The two chat further over a cool bowl of water and determine some things can't be explained—let alone understood.

~ Act 2 ~

N: Later that afternoon, Stephanie remembers a promise she made and asks her timely friend to accompany her to a nearby playground. There she meets her old friend Owl Face and attempts to introduce the two.

Stephanie: Owl Face, meet Eternity. Eternity, Owl Face.

Eternity: Hi! You can call me Father Time if you like.

Owl Face: Who? Who? Ah, Stephanie there's nobody there.

Eternity: Sorry, Stephanie, time is invisible, remember?

Stephanie: Oh right, I forgot. Look, I promised you something, Owl Face. It's buried nearby.

N: A few hundred feet later, the group comes to a halt by a withering oak tree. There, Stephanie begins clawing the ground while Owl Face flies to a branch overhead. Eternity watches and chuckles as something emerges from the hole the kitten has dug.

Stephanie: Here, take it now! You know what to do!

N: The great bird swoops down and snatches the object from Stephy's claw. Ascending several hundred feet in the air, the owl screams out…

Owl Face: You have no idea what this means, friend! If we're lucky, we'll meet back here in an hour to celebrate.

Eternity: Stephanie, I know what he has and where he's going. I was there when you buried the pacifier and I'm going to be at the police station when Owl Face arrives. Owls are wise, but we're going to need human assistance to explain where the child is for the authorities to act in time.

Stephanie: If you saw me bury the item, why didn't you show yourself then? I hid the toy to keep the criminals from retrieving it but couldn't figure out what to do next.

Eternity: Stephy, the parents can't afford the ransom, and those criminals won't hold the baby much longer. In this time period, the police only have DNA samples and fingerprints to help them. Get me your human caretakers, and I'll take it from there.

~ *Act 3* ~

N: Now back home, Stephanie bounds up the back stairs and leaps through the window—landing squarely on poor Beth seated on the couch.

Beth: Stephy! Why do you do that? You scared me to death!

Stephanie *(to herself)*: No time for small talk, GO ANSWER THE DOOR!

N: Beth hears the doorbell chime, but upon opening the door, she simply finds a note.

Beth: Bob, come quick! This was left on the door. What could it mean?

Bob *(reading)*: Everyone thinks there's all the time in the world until they realize there isn't. The infant's parents are frantic, and you must explain the tale. Time waits for no man.

N: And it is signed Chronos.

Bob: Chronos? Explain the tale? This is nuts!

N: Suddenly the radio station they were listening to breaks regular programming for a special bulletin. They hear, "Police are searching the Lowell Field area for the missing three-year-old, more details forthcoming."

Beth: Look, Stephy has something in her mouth. She'll choke! Grab her, Bob!

Bob: Too late! She's out the window again and headed for Lowell Field!

N: The two run after their kitten at full speed but abruptly stop as neither can comprehend the sight before them.

Beth: Do you see what I see? Could that be a glowing hourglass floating above that discarded refrigerator?

Bob: See it, yes; believe it, no. The glow around it is blinding! Say, aren't the doors to these things supposed to be removed for recycle pickup? And what's that muffled crying noise all about?

N: Just then, Stephanie appears, runs around to the front of the refrigerator, and hisses loudly at its door.

Bob: I'll pry open the door, Beth, you grab the kid!

Eternity: Stephanie, the future looks bright for that baby now. You know, I've never interfered with human activity before. Your friend Owl Face is still wondering what happened to the cargo he was carrying to the police station. He'll be very upset with himself I'm sure. Explain it all to him, OK?

N: With that, the hourglass disappears and an old gentleman is seen briskly walking down the street. He then turns a corner and is gone.

Case of the Misplaced Catacombs (Part 1)

Cast

N: Narrator

Stephy, Stephanie: House cat able to speak fluently to all non-human characters

Beth: Stephanie's owner, married to Bob

Bob: Stephanie's owner, married to Beth

Winfred Lee: Mysterious individual, sinister in nature

Tour Guide: Helpful individual, not to be trusted

~*Act 1*~

N: Our story opens half a world away from a little house on Bennett Street. Early September brought the opportunity for travel as Beth's magazine article required firsthand information on Beijing's colorful past.

Beth: Phew, what a flight! Thankfully our hotel accommodations are first rate! Let's rest up and check out their Chinese restaurant downstairs.

Bob: Great! Your editor spared no expense! Private jets and world class hotels? I could get used to this. How about you, Stephy?

Stephy *(to herself)*: Cramped baggage compartments in a cold cargo hold with a dash of turbulence? Sure! What's not to like?

N: A knock on the door and complimentary room service provides a soft pillow and a hearty bowl of sushi for the smallest guest in the room.

Stephy: OK, now I'm happy.

Beth: Oh look, a set of hairbrushes and an exquisite comb! What a marvelous touch! What do you think? Not like home, is it?

Bob: What? Oh sure. When do we eat?

N: While the humans are out to dinner, our favorite sleuth checks out the hotel room. Finding nothing familiar with any of it, she jumps to the windowsill to sulk.

Stephy: Would it have killed them to bring my toys? Hey, what's this?

N: Looking out the window, she observes a hotel employee pulling a set of luggage from a car and placing them onto a cart.

Stephy: Stop! Thief! Don't let him get away! Man, it doesn't matter where I go, trouble is always there ahead of me.

N: Turning from the window, Stephanie paused briefly before jumping to the floor.

Stephy: Ooooh! Nice comb! I'll get back to you later! Now where do they keep their open windows around here?

~Act 2~

N: The next few days were a combination of in town sightseeing and copious note-taking. Beth then decided her article should have a "living history" feel to it.

Bob: How do we obtain a "living history" feel? Do we live in the past?

Beth: Stick to playwriting, Bob. We're off to the mountains where the past comes alive! Everyone, to the bus!

N: It turns out that everyone included Stephanie and a happy group of foreign-speaking tourists from the same hotel. Twenty minutes later, the bus stopped at a grand cabin at the base of a towering mountain range.

Tour guide *(in Cantonese)*: Nanling mountains, Pearl River Basin below. All to cabin now for rest and nourishment!

Bob: What the heck is he saying? Do we have a flat?

Winfred Lee: Allow me to translate. We have arrived, and he wishes everyone to follow him inside.

Beth: Thank you, we are Beth and Bob from America. This is our first trip to your country.

Winfred Lee: I'm Winfred Lee. You've chosen an unusual area to visit. Some believe the spirits of the mountain travel with first-time visitors. Stay close to your guide though, and you'll be fine.

Bob: Is there a danger we're not aware of?

Winfred Lee: Not unless you trespass on sacred ground. The guide will guarantee you safe passage. You have a most interesting animal with you. Good travels to you all.

N: The guide provided adequate time for food and rest before starting out on foot toward a towering waterfall.

Tour guide *(in English)***:** Stay close, everyone. We will hike to the large platform and take the gondola to the summit. Picture-taking in this area is encouraged.

Beth: Bob, did you notice how Stephanie's fur was on end when we met Winfred? She doesn't usually hiss at strangers either.

Bob: I did.

~ Act 3 ~

N: During the ride up the mountainside, the tour guide points out the prominent sights and takes questions from the group.

Bob: I've been told there are spirits here. Are there areas we're forbidden to see?

Tour guide: Who told you that?

Bob: One of the group members on the bus. I don't see him now. He gave his name as Winfred.

Tour guide *(whispering)***:** Winfred Lee? Stay close, friend. Do not lose sight of me.

N: Beth looked down at the kitten she was carrying and noticed the tiny, exquisite comb from the hotel.

Beth: How in the world? Look! Stephy has the comb from the hotel! I can't untangle it from her fur! I guess it's the cat's comb now.

Bob: Leave it. We may have bigger problems.

Tour guide: OK, group! Everyone is free to wander about. Please stay within the roped-off areas. We'll regroup in thirty minutes.

N: Stephy sees something move and jumps from Beth's arms. Running at top speed, she leaps over the roped stanchion and down a steep embankment.

Beth: Bob, grab her! Oh no, she's gone!

N: Despite the tour guide's protests, Beth and Bob quickly follow Stephanie's trail to a grassy area far below. There they notice a hole in the ground with a tiny comb beside it.

Bob *(digging furiously with his hands)***:** Beth, grab that flat rock over there!

N: Working together, they widen the hole in no time. Then, deep within the earth, a low rumbling sound was heard. Seconds later, the two disappear from view.

Case of the Misplaced Catacombs (Part 2)

Cast

N: Narrator

Stephy, Stephanie: House cat able to speak fluently to all non-human characters

Beth: Stephanie's owner, married to Bob

Bob: Stephanie's owner, married to Beth

Winfred Lee: Mysterious individual, sinister in nature

Tour Guide: Helpful individual, not to be trusted

~Act 1~

N: We left Beth and Bob disappearing in the southern Chinese province of Guangxi somewhere near the Nanling Mountains and the Pearl River Basin. Their worried tour guide had called the authorities, and a search party was now being assembled.

Tour Guide: Group! Back to the gondola! We will allow the authorities the area. Follow me please!

Beth: It's incredibly dark down here, Bob. We must have slid a quarter mile down! Are you alright? I can't see a thing.

Bob: Yep, I'm OK! Just a little bruised is all. Let's look around this cavernous place and find little Stephy.

N: Bob walks two feet forward and stumbles into a wall.

Bob: A torch! Hanging right on this wall! Got a match?

N: Luckily, she has a lighter in her purse. When lit, the torch illuminates an incredible scene…

Beth: This place is unreal! Look at the carvings! Could that be a shield against this stone?

N: Further inspection reveals the imperial crest of Rome on the shield and the skeletal remains of a roman legionnaire.

Beth: YIKES, WHAT'S THAT!

Bob: I can't be sure, but I think that's a Roman foot soldier who may have been guarding the place.

Beth: Roman foot soldier? But we're nowhere near Rome!

Bob: Well we know they conquered the area around the Mediterranean Sea. Maybe their Egyptian fleet sailed down the Red Sea and took a left?

Beth: That would be some left! I can't imagine how long a sea voyage that would have been. Why doesn't the world know they were here?

Bob *(pointing to the skeleton)*: Ask him! I'm guessing they never made it home. Let's look around a little more.

Beth: Over here! This rocky ledge was hewn with a tool into the shape of a coffin. The Latin carved into the lid indicates this is the burial site of a wealthy Roman citizen. I've heard of catacombs in both Italy and France but never this far east. What a find! Think of the article I could write!

N: At that point, a kitten's cry can be heard, and around a darkened corner is Stephanie with a small golden bracelet wrapped around a paw.

Beth: She's OK! Let's free her of this and get out of here!

~Act 2~

N: The imprisoned trio found their exiting was to be far more difficult than entering had been. Tons of loose soil and debris had collapsed the entrance, and panic was setting in.

Beth: There's no way out! We're trapped down here forever!

Bob: OK, let's think this through. Our torch is burning just fine, so there must be air getting in from somewhere. The tour guide saw us run off and probably called the authorities. And the collapse would have left quite a mess topside, so finding the entrance would be no problem.

Beth: OK, smartie, how do we get out?

Winfred Lee: That's easy. You don't.

N: Stephanie arched her back and hissed at the figure before her.

Bob: Yeah? Well if we don't, you don't.

Tourist guide: I'm guessing you're wrong there, my friend.

Beth: But how? You were with the group!

Winfred Lee: Did it ever occur to you there might be another way in? Your unfortunate find poses a bit of a problem, but I figure you might want to help us help you.

Bob: Want to run that by us again?

Tourist guide: Yeah! Your cat found some jewelry, I see, and there's plenty more where that came from. We could use a little help gathering it up before you join soldier boy over there.

Bob: Grave robbers! No wonder you told us about trespassing on sacred ground. You didn't want problems and thought you could scare us off!

Beth: The group saw us run off! They'll report us missing! You'll never get away with this.

Tourist guide: You're right, they did. They also saw me contact the authorities before I took them off the mountain. The police will be searching in the wrong area, I assure you.

~ *Act 3* ~

N: While all this human dialogue was progressing, a certain non-human was staying busy. No one saw Stephanie walk away following her nose and sniffing out the fresh air coming from the second entrance.

Stephy: Hey, sunlight! Someone needs to know my caretakers are in trouble. Got to get a plan…

N: Planning was never in Stephanie's skill set. She did however possess common sense (sort of). She remembered seeing a shiny silver plate where the bracelet was and dragged it back to the entrance.

Stephy: It's not one of Mom's mirrors, but it will have to do.

N: Dropping the plate on the ground allowed the sun to reflect a flashing glint that could be seen for miles. Stephanie kept sitting on and getting up from the plate, causing an improbable distress signal to be sent. Luckily, one in the search party caught a glimpse and went over to investigate.

Winfred Lee: There, that just about does it! We'll have enough treasure to retire comfortably, won't we? And remember we can always come back for more.

Bob: I could hold the gun for a while if you want to go back for more.

Winfred Lee: Very funny. OK, you three, over by the soldier.

Tourist guide: You three?

Winfred Lee: Sure, why split the loot when I can have it all?

N: Two shots later, one retirement wannabe lay dead on the ground.

Winfred Lee: What do you think? Ladies first?

N:	The gunshots brought the search party to the entrance in force. Their excited voices echoed off the cavernous walls, causing Winfred to hesitate and rethink his actions.

Winfred Lee: New plan, everybody over there! Hands on your head and keep still!

Bob:	You can't pull the trigger without giving yourself away. They're almost here! Toss the gun on the floor or you'll be the next to kick the bucket.

Winfred Lee: Impudent Americans! Always giving orders!

N:	Winfred momentarily turned toward the approaching rescuers, giving Beth the chance to bean him in the head with a rock. The gun then hit the floor followed by the robber.

Bob:	Wow! Remind me to stay on your good side.

The Academy

Cast

N: Narrator

Stephy, Stephanie: House cat able to speak fluently to all non-human characters

Beth: Stephanie's owner, married to Bob

Bob: Stephanie's owner, married to Beth

Administrator: Head of Santa Claws Reform School for Kittens

Mansfield: Administrative assistant

Cherub: Friend of Stephanie

~*Act 1*~

N: Our story opens in a little house on Bennett Street. The early morning hours of a beautiful spring day are shattered by a series of crashes emanating from the kitchen.

Beth: WHAT'S THAT NOISE?!

Bob: I'm not sure, but it doesn't sound good. Go back to sleep, I'll check it out.

Stephy: There! Finally some counter space for my window-viewing pleasure. Now where were we? Oh yeah, the birdies.

Bob *(approaching the disaster)***:** Stephy! Bad kitten! Get off the counter NOW!

N: Startled by the rude interruption, Stephy jumps down, taking the toaster with her. She then proceeds to step up her game in the living room.

Stephy: Really? I'm going to have to teach them proper kitten pampering procedures. Right after I destroy these drapes.

Beth: My drapes! Bad kitten! Shoooo!

N: Not in the mood to shoooo, Stephy stubbornly digs her claws into the window screen taking care to rip them apart as well.

Beth: Ahhhh! What are we going to do with you?

Stephy *(to herself)***:** Give me treats?

Beth: Bob! Get that cat out of the house NOW!

N: Banished to the backyard for the tiniest of infractions, the sulking kitten moves on to the bird feeders and shatters them nicely.

Bob: I hate to say this, but she's going to need kitten training classes.

Beth: Right! I'll make the call! See if you can locate her traveling baskets!

~*Act 2*~

N: The following Monday, a caged Stephanie was carted off to the Santa Claws Reform School for Kittens. Upon arriving, the trio is invited into the administrator's office for a pre-admission interview.

Administrator: Welcome! I'm sure you have questions, but first let me ask, What seems to be the problem?

Beth: I don't know how to put this, but she's not your typical feline. Lately she's adopted a destructive trait never before seen on the planet.

Administrator: I see. Well here at SCRSFK, our policy is simply that there are no bad kittens—only misunderstood ones.

Stephy *(from behind bars)*: Yeah! Listen to him! I'm misunderstood!

Bob: You mean to say our cat's behavior will improve when we do?

Administrator: Right! Here at the Academy, we take a holistic approach. Our training includes the entire family. Both the physical and mental aspects of each member are taken into account. When would you like to start?

N: Beth and Bob exchange looks and start to rise from their seats when…

Mansfield: Excuse me, sir, sorry to interrupt, but we have a situation. Gates two and three have been breached. I'm afraid your immediate attention is required.

Administrator: Both two and three? Stay with these kind folks, Mansfield. I'll be back momentarily.

N: The administrator's abrupt departure gave Bob the opportunity to pick up Stephanie's pet carrier and head for the door. Beth was in the process of leaving as well when…

Mansfield: Please, sir, don't open that door!

Bob: Too late, we're out of here! Beth why don't we…YIKES!

N: The open door allows several dozens of rampaging loose cats entrance into the room. Mansfield ducks behind a couch, Beth screams something unprintable, and Bob being closest to the hall is simply run over. Stephanie's cage flies into a desk and pops open.

Mansfield *(into a microphone)***:** Mayday! Mayday! Seal off all exterior exits!

~ *Act 3* ~

N: Leaderless, the kitten tsunami again sweeps out into the hall with one additional recruit. While the humans pick themselves up off the floor, we hear…

Stephy: Name's Stephy. Where are we going?

Cherub: Don't know. (Huff puff) I'm new. Looking for a way out!

Stephy: Follow me, gang! We'll go out the way I came in!

N: Suddenly their unelected leader is leading the charge!

Stephy: Watch for open windows! Check any loose cabinet doors for food cans! I've got humans willing to help the cause!

Cherub: This hallway looks familiar! Way to go, Stephy! WAIT!

N: The charge comes to a sudden halt as men with nets block the way.

Stephy: The outside world is just beyond those goons! Listen up! I've got a plan. You ten on the left, jump up on the counters. You twelve on the right, swoop through and bite their legs, the rest of you follow my lead and scratch them from their waist up. Great work, guys! Counter kittens, jump down on their shoulders! Survivors, meet me at the door!

N: Amid hissing cats, swinging nets, and a lot of random biting, the two humans go down. Meanwhile, Stephy used her considerable talents in doorknob turning, allowing the group access to the facility's parking lot.

Stephy: Run for it! Scatter! They can't catch us all!

Cherub: Wow! Do you do this for a living?

N: Beth and Bob follow the carnage to their car. Seeing Stephanie, they scoop her up and jump into their vehicle. Bob tries steering around the wave of furry demons toward the relative safety of the highway while Mansfield is in the process of remotely closing the parking lot's main gate.

Bob: Hang on tight! This is going to be close!

N: Stephanie removes her paws from her eyes in time to see Cherub on top of the closing gate. With a smile on her lips, Cherub jumps to a nearby tree branch, bending it enough to catch the gate's latch!

Bob: There might be enough room! We're through!

Beth: What should we do with the rest of our day?

The Dollhouse Caper

Cast

N: Narrator

Stephy, Stephanie: House cat able to speak fluently to all non-human characters

Beth: Stephanie's owner, married to Bob

Bob: Stephanie's owner, married to Beth

Little Girl: Customer shopping with her mother

Mother: Customer shopping with her daughter

Announcer: Store employee making storewide announcements

Security Officer: Store employee

~Act 1~

N: Our story opens in a strange location for Stephanie. Never before has she seen such a huge building or been so far from home.

Beth: There's a parking space, Bob! Quick, pull in there!

N: Bob navigates through a sea of abandoned shopping carts and package-laden pedestrians only to arrive too late. Two minivans converge upon the location seconds before Bob's arrival.

Bob: I'll circle around again and let you out at the mall's entrance.

N: The process takes longer than expected, prompting Beth to say...

Beth: Christmas is still two weeks away, why did they pick now to shop? Wouldn't online shopping have been easier?

Bob: Yep! Tell you what though, the experience just wouldn't have been the same.

N: Beth jumps out at the door and runs right into a donation kettle. Somehow the experience isn't making the grade. Meanwhile Bob has found parking at the far end of the lot.

Bob: Stephanie, you're coming with me. It's just too cold to leave you in the car. I should have thought to bring a leash.

Stephanie: What? A leash? Bad enough we went to the vet's office first, and now they're thinking of typing me up? The cold has numbed his brain!

N: Bob simply tucks Stephanie inside his overcoat and sprints across the parking lot. Finding Beth and an empty shopping cart, they head for the store's toy section.

Beth: What's become of Stephy?

Bob: She's closer than you think. Check the lining of my coat.

Stephanie *(feeling bashed and bruised)*: I'm going to scratch him to pieces! No way he's coming out of this alive. Wow, is it warm in here—and bright!

N: Stephanie's eyes quickly adjust to the light. Suddenly, before Bob can react, she leaps to the top shelf of the toy rack and blends in with the rows of stuffed animals.

~Act 2~

N: Beth and Bob frantically search for Stephanie but to no avail. Thinking she may have gone to the pet food aisle, they begin a thorough search of that area.

Beth: She's not here either. What are we going to do?

Bob: Let's see if the store will put out a public notification on their public address system. How should we best describe her?

N: While our pet owners decide on the wording, Stephanie has moved on to the dollhouse displays. Finding one to her liking, she settles in only to hear…

Announcer: Your attention please. A tiger-striped kitten has been reported lost within the store. A large reward for her safe return to the courtesy booth has been posted. Thank you for your kind attention.

Beth: All we can do now is wait! Things can't get much worse! What more can we do?

Bob: Didn't we come here to shop?

Beth: Bob!

N:　　　　Meanwhile elsewhere in the store…

Little Girl: Mommy, Mommy! I want that dollhouse!

Mother:　We'll see, dear, let's check the box and see what we have here.

N:　　　　Upon taking the partially opened box down, she says…

Mother:　Oh, the box has been opened and its heavier than I thought.

N:　　　　With the carton now safely in the shopping basket, mother and child peer inside the box. Staring back at them are two large unblinking eyes accompanied by a loud hissing sound.

Little Girl: Look! It comes with its own house cat. Can we buy it?

~ *Act 3* ~

N:　　　　The shrieking mother scares poor Stephanie out of her sanctuary and draws the attention of shoppers all over the store. Soon the peaceful shopping atmosphere changes into a mob seeking to cash in on the reward. Stephanie, sensing her life is in danger, darts from aisle to aisle looking for a way out. Store security tries to calm the crowd, but their presence only adds to the drama.

Beth:　　What is going on over there? Look at that craziness!

Bob:　　Must be a special sale. Look, it's happening in the toy aisle!

N:　　　　Once again the public address system comes to life.

Announcer: Ladies and gentlemen, shoppers, your attention please! The kitten has been found. Please continue your shopping and enjoy an additional ten percent off at checkout!

Beth: Bob did you hear? They've found Stephanie!

N: Stephanie, scared out of her wits, has found shelter in the front of the store. Seeing Beth and Bob approach the courtesy booth, she flies into Beth's arms shaking and crying. The media alerted to the event starts taking pictures of the reunion and interviews everyone. The next few minutes though would be hard to explain.

Security Officer: Is she yours?

Bob: I'm afraid so.

Security Officer: Come with me please.

N: Store management explains store policy against pets on the premises. They further explain the additional discount at checkout was a loss in profits for the store but was thought necessary to maintain order. Bob counters by explaining the customers appreciated the savings and it would lead to repeat business. Also the publicity the incident created brought positive attention to the store. It was then determined no real harm had been done. The store's promotional department wanted to know if Stephanie's picture could be purchased for advertising with a gift card thrown in.

Beth: For sure!

The Transformation

Cast

N: Narrator

Stephy, Stephanie: House cat able to speak fluently to all non-human characters

Beth: Stephanie's owner, married to Bob

Bob: Stephanie's owner, married to Beth

Genie: Magical individual

~Act 1~

N: Our story opens in a little house on Bennett Street. Mild spring weather has prompted Beth to start the annual gardening ritual of her pointing a finger and Bob digging furiously to keep up.

Beth: OK, let's see now. The vegetables are planted nicely. How about extending things a bit and putting in a flower bed? What do you think, Stephy?

Stephy *(to herself)*: I think you've trained him well. Hey, what's this?

N: Stephanie noses over to a small lamp Bob has unearthed, then rubs against it to relieve an itch. Suddenly a soft whisper within says…

Genie: Roll the lamp under the bush.

Beth: OK, let's take a break for a few minutes. How about some iced tea?

N: With the humans inside, Stephanie rolls the lamp as instructed and watches in amazement as a figure materializes before her.

Genie: I thought they'd never leave! OK, how about those wishes?

Stephy: What wishes?

Genie: You know, your three wishes! Don't you read fairytales?

Stephy: Nope, can't say I do. Tell me more though, it sounds good.

Genie: Why do I always get the rookies? Look, you rubbed the lamp, and I grant you three wishes. It's really not that complicated. What do you want first?

Stephy: Well, I'd like to be human for a while and live with Beth and Bob.

Genie: Done! You're an exchange student from a foreign land. You work out the details. Call me when you're ready with wish number two.

N: The genie made the humans decide to offer housing for students from the local university to facilitate the first wish.

Bob: Thanks for the tea! When do you think that foreign student will arrive?

Beth: Next week! I can't wait to see what Stephy does with a stranger living among us!

~Act 2~

N: The time passes quickly, and one weekend morning, Stephanie starts to feel strange in the backyard. A mist swirls around her accompanied by a flash of light, then…

Stephy: Wow! I'm taller than ever, and I can speak! I think I'll go around and ring the doorbell now that I can reach it

Beth: That's the door, I'll get it!

N: As the door opens a beautiful young lady with mysterious golden eyes holds out her hand in greeting.

Stephy: Hi, I'm Stephanie, pleased to meet you!

Beth: Hi, are you the exchange student we were expecting?

Stephy: Yes, I'm taking animal husbandry at the university.

Beth: Bob! Come meet Stephanie, our exchange student!

Bob: Hi, please come in! How about a little lunch?

Stephy: Great! I'm sure you have many questions.

Beth: Where's home?

Stephy: Catalina, Egypt, not far from the pyramids.

N: Through the course of the meal, Beth and Bob are treated to a fantastic story of travel and intrigue. Beth notices her guest is simply drinking water and says…

Beth: Not hungry? Is it the time difference?

Stephy: Yes, I'm sure that's it. Would you excuse me while I settle in?

Beth: Sure! The guest room is at the top of the stairs on the right.

Stephy: I know, I'll see you in a little while. I'm in need of a cat nap after my trip.

~ *Act 3* ~

N: A week has past and our hosts have noticed some peculiarities concerning their guest. They also can't seem to find their pet anywhere. The usual search patterns have turned up nothing, and wanted posters are once again all over the neighborhood offering a reward for her return.

Beth: Stephy hasn't brought home books or asked to have people over to study since she has arrived. Do you think she's well? And she seems to sleep a lot during the day in the oddest places. Should we have a talk with her?

Bob: No, she is probably shy or used to a very different lifestyle. It is strange to see her asleep on the living room rug in a pool of sunlight every afternoon though. Maybe we could take her out to see the Boston area sights. It might help us relieve our worries as well.

N: The group decides to take a duck boat tour of the city the following day. All goes well until a soft growl is heard.

Stephy: The lady behind us has a dog! We've got to get off the boat!

Beth: It's a seeing eye dog, Stephy. They're very well trained. You'll be alright. Look, the Museum of Science!

N: With all eyes on the building, a sudden splash is heard on the other side of the boat!

Bob: Man overboard! Stop the boat! Help me with the life preserver!

Beth: She's gone! She never came up again for air! Did the current grab her? Where could she be?

N: Meanwhile, under the surface, Stephy has made a second wish.

Stephy: I'm through with this human stuff, put me back in my body and send me home!

Genie: Granted!

N: A very distraught Beth and Bob report the incident to the police and a rescue effort is made to no avail. Returning home, they discover a wet Stephanie drying in the living room sunlight wrapped up in a scarf her former self was wearing.

Beth: We've lost both Stephanies and… look!

N: Beth faints and falls to the floor. Bob rushes to her side and dials 911. Stephanie takes in the scene and thinks about calling her genie for a third time

Bob: Beth! Are you alright? The paramedics say your vital signs are fine, but rest. I'll see to Stephy.

N: Bob finds Stephy has retreated to the guest room. There he finds dozens of opened cat food cans and boxes of catnip stored in a corner. Confused, he looks at Stephy and says…

Bob: What is all this? We didn't buy anything here. All these cat collars have your body with our exchange student's face engraved on them. Beth, come in here. There's something you've got to see!

N: Thinking quickly, Stephanie calls upon the genie for her third wish.

Stephy: MAKE THEM FORGET EVERYTHING NOW! NONE OF THIS EVER HAPPENED.

Genie: Done! Don't call me again! Ever! Me and the lamp are out of here!

Beth *(arriving at the door)***:** What is it, Bob? Stephy looks comfortable in the sunlight curled up on the rug, doesn't she?

Yesterday's Tomorrow

Cast

N: Narrator

Stephy, Stephanie: House cat able to speak fluently to all non-human characters

Beth: Stephanie's owner, married to Bob

Bob: Stephanie's owner, married to Beth

Pierre Dupree: French Patriot

~Act 1~

N:	Our story opens in an old graveyard blocks away from Bennett Street. Winter's blanket of white has given way to spring's carpet of green. Stephanie enters looking for a friend but finds…
Stephy:	Pierre, where are you? It's getting late, I've got to get home!
N:	Three graves over, a mist rises and a voice answers…
Pierre:	Here! Come closer and be recognized.
Stephy:	Pierre? That doesn't sound like you! What are you wearing? I can see right through you!
Pierre:	I am Pierre but perhaps not the one you seek. The uniform I wear displays my rank of captain in the French Advance Guard of King Louis XV.
Stephy:	Wow! What are you doing here? Why are you shimmering so?
Pierre:	Alas, this is the location of my final resting place. I passed in the year 1755.
Stephy:	You passed? You mean died? That would make you a ghost, right?
Pierre:	Correct. Let me formally introduce myself. I'm Captain Pierre Dupree, and you are?
Stephy:	Stephy. Still living, by the way. How did you die?
Pierre:	The English! That impudent General Edward Braddock encroaching on land claimed by France. I was to fall in an engagement led by that upstart twenty-three-year-old Lieutenant Colonel George Washington.
Stephy:	Yeah? The guy on the dollar bill? Were you shot?
Pierre:	No, bayonetted while cresting a hill. What's a dollar bill?
Stephy:	Money, of course. Look, I've got to go.
Pierre:	Don't leave me, they always leave me.

~*Act 2*~

N: Stephanie arrived at home just as the sun set. Her food dish ready, she settled in and finally came to rest in the living room. Bob was watching a documentary on the History Channel concerning the French and Indian War. To his amazement, Stephy jumped right up onto his lap and really seemed to be intently watching the screen.

Bob: Beth! Come quick, you've got to see this!

Beth: What is it? WOW, Stephy looks like she's studying for finals!

Stephy (*thinking loudly*): Quiet! I've got to learn this for Pierre Dupree! He's gonna want to know how everything turned out!

N: Later, the following evening, Stephanie again visited the old neighborhood graveyard. Upon arriving at Dupree's headstone, she witnessed the now familiar mist rising up from the plot.

Stephy: Hi, glad I caught you in. I've got news!

Pierre: OK, what's the news?

Stephy: I know what happens in your war!

Pierre: You mean you know the outcome? What are you, clairvoyant?

Stephy: I don't think so. Hey, do you just talk to me or do others stop by?

Pierre: Well, there are a few now and then, but they're dressed so strangely I never speak to them. You're dressed in a more traditional trapper's outfit of furs with a raccoon's cap featuring the tail off the back I admire so much. You do however seem shorter than most.

Stephy: Yeah, sure. I take it you can't see all that well, huh?

Pierre: Not really, you're kind of blurry, sort of misty really. Anyway I'm more at ease with you. But back to the war, how do you know what happens? When I left the field, it was a toss-up as to how it might end.

Stephy: Well here in 2019, we have specials on TV and I caught one last night.

Pierre: Right! What the heck are you talking about? The year 2019 is some 264 years in the future. Are you a spirit of what's to come?

N: The two discuss the war and its outcome. Pierre is delighted to find the English later lost their colonies and changes his mind about George Washington and his role in all this. Stephanie let it slip that history had forgotten Pierre and then hit upon an even more delicate topic.

Stephy: The ambush you led took place in what is now western Pennsylvania. How did you end up getting buried here?

~ *Act 3* ~

N: Pierre related his final wish on the battlefield was to be buried at sea. He grew ever more agitated at the prospect of never seeing France again and as his anger increased, the surrounding area suffered his wrath.

Stephy *(feeling the ground shake)*: Easy, big guy! Headstones are cracking here. Calm yourself. I might be able to help.

Pierre: At least tell me where this place is located. My command was to head east to the Dutch settlement of New Amsterdam. That area, having been turned over to the English one hundred years earlier, was ripe for revolution with a strong underground resistance in place. French reinforcements were coming in by sea, and we stood a good chance of ridding ourselves of the enemy altogether.

Stephy: New Amsterdam is today's New York City. I'm thinking you would have returned to France on a French warship then?

Pierre: Right! Or burial at sea if I passed earlier than expected.

Stephy: Well you fell short. We're about ten miles west of Boston in a town named Waltham.

Pierre *(thundering)***:** Boston! That lousy English backwater port? And Waltham, you say? Like Waltham Abbey town in England? Egads!

N: Horrified Stephy watches the ground split open above the grave. The motion forces an urn to the surface with the inscription "French Patriot Pierre Dupree—return me home to my beloved Marseille 1755." Moments later, several cemetery ground keepers appeared, scooped up Stephy and the urn, and returned to their office. The media was alerted to the event and found Stephanie to be the agent for Pierre's last request to come to volition. A news story on the six o'clock broadcast featured a GoFundMe page and a taped interview with Stephy and the ground keepers.

Bob *(watching the news)***:** Beth! You've got to see this!

Sherlock Stephy

Cast

N: Narrator

Stephy, Stephanie: House cat able to speak fluently to all non-human characters

Beth: Stephanie's owner, married to Bob

Bob: Stephanie's owner, married to Beth

Detectives #1, #2, #3: Waltham Police special investigation unit

~Act 1~

N: An evening murder has taken place down by the river. The crime scene tape was already in place when Stephanie strolled out of her yard on Bennett Street intent on a late-evening walk in the moonlight.

Detective #1: How long has he been there? Any identification on the body? Hey, shine that light over here!

Detective #2: About two hours I'd say, no wallet on him. Whatcha looking at on the bank over there?

Detective #1: Footprints in the mud moving away from the scene. Have the patrolmen follow the trail. Those fallen leaves won't help much.

N: At this point, Stephanie emerges from the woods, frightening the searching officers in the process. Recoiling, she hisses as her eyes wickedly reflect back the flashlight's beams.

Detective #1: It's just a cat! Concentrate, men, we have a case to solve.

Stephy: A case? Hey, I want to play!

Detective #2: Right! Search around for clues! We'll have early morning joggers here soon messing things up for sure.

N: Stephanie's keen eyes were well adjusted for night vision. Watching the humans, she ascertained the game had something to do with finding something. Looking at the ground before her, she spotted a shiny object, picked it up, and dropped it at the detective's feet.

Detective #1: What have we here? A bullet casing? Good kitten!

N: The next few minutes again thoroughly perplexed the officers. Stephanie leaped to a nearby tree and pulled down a scarf dangling from a high branch.

Detective #2: What's this? Look! The scarf matches the victim's jacket! Man, what is she doing now?

N: Stephanie had launched herself from the tree to an object floating just offshore. Clamping down upon the soggy mess, she swam to the riverbank and dropped it on a rock.

Detective #1: Now what? A bloodstained handkerchief! Wow!

N: An officer reached for the kitten and barely glimpsed the phone number on the collar before she ran off.

~Act 2~

N: The following morning, Beth received a recorded message on her phone from the local precinct.

Beth: Bob! Stephy is wanted by the police!

Bob: Should I get a lawyer?

Beth: No. At least I don't think so. She's wanted in connection with a murder investigation. They emphatically requested her presence at headquarters this afternoon. She's to report to the detective's division.

Bob: I've got a bad feeling about this.

N: Several hours later, all are at the station seated in the squad situation room.

Detective #1: Thank you all for coming. I'll make this brief. The department would appreciate the loan of your kitten for the next few hours.

Beth: Is she being investigated?

Detective #2: No, nothing like that. She was most helpful last night in obtaining evidence pertaining to a recent homicide. We would like to make her the lead—a sort of honorary police bloodhound if you will. You'll be paid for her time.

Bob: Stephy? The lead investigator? Is this for real?

Detective #1: I assure you it is. The police consider her an asset. Just sign this release and we'll put her in the field immediately.

N: And so the asset along with half the detectives on the force returned to the scene of the crime. Full daylight was to reveal further evidence of foul play.

Detective #3: I'm opening the pet carrier now. Keep her in sight at all times! Mark any location where she may linger as well.

Stephy: Free at last! Let's get to work here! Follow me!

~ *Act 3* ~

N: Like an arrow shot from a bow, Stephanie ran toward the river and stopped. She sniffed the air, turned left, and proceeded to scratch the underside of the riverbank. The detectives followed closely.

Detective #1 *(pointing)***:** You! Dig here! Everyone else, follow that kitten!

Detective #2: She's on the move again! She's going the wrong way!

N: Stephanie left the crime scene entirely. Her rapid travels took her up and over the rise and across the bike path. Two hundred feet into the woods, she again stopped and looked upward. A low growling sound came down from above.

Fugitive: Get away, cat! Beat it!

Detective#3: Over here! The murder weapon was buried in the riverbank.

N: All went left. The fugitive climbed down from the tree and went right!

Detective #2: Could be the weapon used! The shell casing Stephy found was a .38 caliber and so is the gun. Let's get it back to the lab for fingerprints. Where's that cat?

Stephy: Outrun me will you? I don't think so.

N: Stephanie leaped up and scratched the fugitive's face. Bleeding above the eye, the panicked man blindly ran through the woods leaving behind a well-marked trail. Stephy knew she needed human assistance and stopped dead in her tracks.

Detective #1: I see her! She's over by the rocks! Hey! She's got fresh blood on her fur!

Detective #2: Right! Look, a fresh trail veering off to the right. Let's go!

N: Less than a hundred yards away lay a figure on the ground mopping his face with a handkerchief matching the one from the day before. A search of the suspect produced a wallet with the victim's identification inside.

Detective #1: We have our man. Get an ambulance. He's pretty badly scratched up. We'll book him later. Let's return Stephy. I'm sure the press will have a field day with this one!

Stephanie and the Mystery of the Emerald Stone

Cast

N: Narrator

Stephy, Stephanie: House cat able to speak fluently to all non-human characters

Beth: Stephanie's owner, married to Bob

Bob: Stephanie's owner, married to Beth

Jeweler: Upstanding professional gone bad

Butler: Gore Estate employee

Guide: Gore Estate employee

~Act 1~

N: Our story begins to unravel in a little house on Bennett Street. It's a cool, rainy day in early April when Beth and Bob arrive home.

Beth: Bob, come quick. I'm in the front hall closet.

Stephy: Hey, I thought I was the only one who stayed there.

Bob: What is it, Beth?

Beth: I was just putting away my coat when I came across this!

Bob: Wow, I've never seen anything like this before. It seems to be some kind of ancient lockbox with savage claw marks on it.

N: Our inquisitive group takes the box to the living room for a better look.

Beth: It was up on the top shelf behind the hats and gloves.

Bob: You know, I bet I could pry it open with my claw hammer.

N: With a flash, Bob is gone. With a zoom, Bob is back. And after a few prying attempts…

Beth and Bob: Will you look at this!

N: Stephy already up on the coffee table peers over the side…

Stephy: Now what kind of a silly human would put the treasure and the map in the same box?

Bob: 1809? This is a bloodstained, 200-year-old map with an emerald!

Beth: Yikes! No, no, it's way too creepy. Let's just put it all back.

Bob: I don't know. That gem must be worth a pretty penny, and the map has a clue or two for me and you.

Stephy *(slapping her forehead)***:** Who writes his material?

N: As it happened, the next day was Saturday. Instead of the usual chores, our group was fast upon a 200-year-old trail.

Bob: Let's start with an appraisal at the local jewelry store.

N: They do so and quickly find the dust-covered gem was nothing to sneeze at.

Jeweler: This emerald is a famous heirloom dating back to our federalist. It's priceless, and it has the most disturbing history.

Beth: Oh, I knew we should've put it back.

Stephy: We're rich I tell you! Rich, rich, rich!

Bob: Ummm. How bad is the story?

Jeweler: Well, according to legend, this was part of a set worn to a gala event by Rebecca Gore when her husband Christopher first became governor of Massachusetts.

Stephy: Yeah, yeah, go back to the cash talk.

Beth: Was this at the Gore Estate? That place is still gorgeous.

Bob: OK, so what happened at the party?

Jeweler: Well someone or something decided to steal the necklace this gem was set in, and in the most mysterious way.

Stephy: Aha! Keep talking!

Jeweler: The party was to be at night in the grand ballroom, which then was illuminated by candlelight and fireplaces. As the guests arrived, they were individually announced and escorted into the room.

Bob: OK, then what?

Jeweler: Well, no one can be sure, but when Rebecca and Christopher entered, a strong, cold breeze blew into the room, blowing out all candles and fires and plunging the entire place into darkness.

Beth: What time of year was this? Who was wearing the necklace?

Jeweler: That's the thing. It was a hot summer's night, and the hostess, Rebecca Gore, wore the necklace into the room.

Bob: What happened next? Why can't anyone be sure?

Jeweler: The outside temperature was nearly 90° when the lights went out. And, well, did I mention the unworldly sounds they heard?

N: The jeweler finishes the story saying…

Jeweler: Rebecca shot her hands up to her throat while her guests nearly trampled each other leaving the mansion in their panicked hurry.

Bob: I know. The necklace was gone!

N: A shaken Beth and Bob then took Stephanie to the Gore Estate itself to learn more.

Beth: Bob, he said this was no prank. People got hurt! The stone must go to the police. Besides, it's haunted.

Bob: No one said anything about ghosts, Beth.

N: Bob's right for once, but even Stephanie is thinking she only has nine lives. The trio arrives at the estate and sounds the enormous brass knocker at its entrance.

Guide: Yes, you're early for the tour, but please wait in the drawing room. Someone will be in shortly with tea.

~Act 2~

Stephy *(thinking aggressively)*: Spill the story, chump, and remember, just the facts, Jack!

N: Settling in, Beth and Bob glance around the lavish room while Stephanie checks under the rug.

Butler: Your tea. Will there be anything else?

Bob: Yes, we're wondering if you might solve a riddle?

Butler: Oh?

Beth: We would like to know about the estate's first party and what really happened that night.

Butler: Oh, yes! You mean the gala. Most interesting but a little ahead of my time.

Bob: Right! Where are the clues? Why are the facts unknown? Who got the goods?

Butler: Well, 200 years would make it a bit of a cold case. I do know the necklace minus its emerald ended in that tree.

N: Beth and Bob glance out the window to view a centuries-old tree some seventy feet high.

Bob: Was the tree that tall back then?

Butler: Oh my, yes! Actually, you see it's been hit by lightning many times since then, oddly always on or about the gala's anniversary. Some say the guest's ghosts are unhappy.

Beth: Gulp. Tell me, are there pictures of the stone?

Butler: Why yes. In the great room within a volume on the mantel.

N: As the Butler fades off, Beth and Bob race to the fireplace followed closely by the curious Stephanie.

Beth: Bob, this is it! Our gem is identical to the book. The lockbox is pictured but oh… check out page seven.

Bob: The guide and the butler. How could they be in this ancient volume and still be here today?

N: At that point, Bob looks down and sees the fur on Stephanie's back standing on its end. Ice is forming on his tea, and Beth is turning a wonderful shade of blue.

Beth: It's cold, so cold. Everything is freezing up.

N: Just then, the room goes totally dark. Stranger still, a powerful breeze passes through the room.

Beth: What's going on?

N: In response, an unseen but familiar set of voices speaks.

Butler: Place the emerald on the table.

Jeweler: Everyone remains where they are.

Guide: Drop the map onto the chair.

Jeweler: Tell us where the lockbox is.

N: Swirls of mist suddenly fill the room when next we hear…

Bob: OK, Beth, now!

N: Out from Beth's shoulder bag comes a powerful flashlight, and before anyone's eyes can adjust…

Stephy: Aha! Attack us… I don't think so!

N: Quickly, Stephanie lunges at the jeweler's hand on the dry ice machine behind the couch. Bam! Two free standing fans are kicked by Bob toward the perpetrator's positions. While…

Beth: Another move and the emerald will be smashed into the fireplace!

N: All freeze in place when suddenly the police rush in, placing handcuffs on the hoodlums.

Jeweler: What's this? How could you have known?

Bob: Cell call to the police on the way over here! You seemed too well informed and desperate to scare us off!

N: A police search of the premises finds the real staff tied up in the basement. They are all more than ready to press charges as well.

Bob: You know, there's still one thing I can't understand.

Beth: Which is?

Bob: How did the lockbox get into our apartment?

N: A purring sound turns everyone's attention to the smallest creature in the room. Scratching furiously, she leaves claw marks upon the table she is perched on—identical to the ones on the lockbox.

For Meowing out Loud

Cast

N: Narrator

Stephy, Stephanie: House cat able to speak fluently to all non-human characters

Beth: Stephanie's owner, married to Bob

Bob: Stephanie's owner, married to Beth

Alice: Beth's piano student

Master of Ceremonies: Head of student performances

~ Act 1 ~

N: Our story opens in a little house on Bennett Street. Beautiful summer weather has made spirits soar, and all are going about their day in their anything-but-routine fashion.

Beth: My two o'clock appointment should be arriving soon. How about taking Stephanie out back for a while?

Bob: Sure! Come on, Stephanie, we've been banished to the yard.

N: The doorbell then chimes, and Beth puts down her sheet music to answer it.

Beth: Come in, Alice! You're right on time!

N: Together they cross over to the living room where the upright piano waits in the corner.

Beth: Shall we pick up where we left off last time? Make yourself comfortable and I'll get the music sheets!

Alice: My recital is only three weeks away! Do you think I'll be ready?

Beth: Are you kidding? You're ready now!

N: As if on cue, a crash in the yard disrupts the lesson long enough for them to hear…

Bob: Sorry! Stephy just plowed into the back door! I think she wants water; it'll just be a minute.

Beth: OK, Alice, let's start the lesson with "Close To You" by the Carpenters!

N: Music filled the air causing Stephanie's ears to rise.

Stephy: What is that noise? Sounds like some kind of party! Why wasn't I invited? Better check this out.

N: A flash later, Stephanie is on top of the piano and settled in for the duration. They are lucky to have her there after all.

~Act 2~

N: Giving in to the inevitable, Beth allowed the listening audience to remain, and the lesson continued.

Alice: You know, I think her head is swaying to the music! You don't think she has hidden talent, do you?

Beth: Maybe, but she usually displays it by accident. Continue, Alice.

Stephy: This party needs a lift! I think vocals are needed.

N: Without further ado, the two humans were treated to a series of meows, which believe it or not, were in concert with the music!

Beth: I can't believe it! Bob! You have to hear this!

N: Bob, carrying a dish of water, enters the room witnessing two wide-eyed pianists and a very vocal kitten.

Bob: What's up with that?

Alice: She's doing it on her own! Has she had lessons too?

Beth: OK, Stephy, let's see if you know the next tune!

N: Another set of meows, though a little off-key, accompanied Alice's version of "Let It Be" by the Beatles. Both Beth and Bob are dumbfounded by the display and ask Alice to play "Happy Birthday."

Alice: She's done it again! Can she join me on stage at the recital?

N: Our cat owners shrug simultaneously and give permission knowing deep inside things probably won't go according to plan.

~ Act 3 ~

N: The day of the recital finally arrives and an audience of parents fills the high school's auditorium. Many student performances precede Alice's debut, and Beth and Bob try to keep Stephanie in check. When the time is right, a spotlight illuminates Alice at the piano with her most accomplished vocalist seated on top.

Master of Ceremonies: And now, ladies and gentlemen, our featured performance. May I present Alice and her wonder cat!

N: The hushed audience holds its collective breath as Alice begins to play. No one is more surprised than Beth and Bob that things have gone this well to date. Three bars into the song and a kitten's meowing can be heard. Paws around the microphone, Stephy looks down at Alice and sort of sings "Fly Me To The Moon" on-key and in time!

Alice: That was great, Stephy, take a bow!

N: Stephanie, being anything but modest, stands on her hind legs and bows gracefully from on top the piano. Unfortunately, the thunderous applause from the audience brings about an entirely different reaction from the kitten. A flash and she is a puffed-up, frazzled mess on top of Alice's head. A heartbeat later, and she leaps to the master of ceremony's podium and shrieks into the live microphone. Beth runs on stage to keep the carnage to a minimum with Bob close behind.

Beth: It's alright, Stephy! Come to mommy! Well get you out of here!

Bob *(grabbing the microphone)*: Your attention please. If we can remain calm, Stephy and Alice will take their final bows!

N: Having nestled in Beth's arms, a calmer Stephanie is placed on the piano once more and indeed curtsies with Alice as the curtain closes. Orchestral music then starts to play "On With The Show" while our group hustles Stephanie off stage. Beth and Bob suggest an ice cream celebration at their house for Alice and her parents, and the singer gets extra helpings of her favorite treats. Don't you wish every day went this well?

Psychic Connection

Cast

N: Narrator

Stephy, Stephanie: House cat able to speak fluently to all non-human characters

Beth: Stephanie's owner, married to Bob

Bob: Stephanie's owner, married to Beth

Psychiatrist: Corporate-sponsored professional

~*Act 1*~

N: Our story opens in a little house on Bennett Street. Late winter weather has all housebound, and spirits are low.

Beth: More snow in the forecast. When will it end?

Bob: Let's do an indoor thing! How about charades? Can you guess what I am?

Stephy: You really want to know? How childish! When boredom looms, I say, go for the catnip!

Beth: Stephy seems happy with her new catnip mousey. How about a glass of wine? We can all enjoy the evening at home!

N: A settling fire in the fireplace, soft music, and good conversation did make for a delightful end of day, but…

Stephy: Whoa! What's in this catnip mousey? Talk about a good batch! I've got to have more of this!

N: Hallucinations abound in a tiny cat brain and when the haze clears…

Bob: I've suddenly got the urge to open cans of cat food!

Beth: Yeah? I'm feeling like opening windows all over the house! What's come over us?

Stephy: Mind control! I'm communicating with you telepathically! Call for more pet supplies to be delivered! I'll require constant pampering!

Bob: Don't know, but I'll tell you this, I'm developing an aversion to dogs!

N: Over the course of the next two weeks, the little house on Bennett Street received an enormous amount of pet-related deliveries. So much so that neighbors were beginning to wonder about the inhabitants there.

~*Act 2*~

N: Both Beth and Bob became uncharacteristically lazy at work, taking frequent unscheduled breaks and dwelling on non-work related concepts. In each case, their superiors called them in to correct the behavior, expecting immediate results. A medical examination was suggested followed by a psych eval at corporate expense.

Psychiatrist: I'm given to understand some purring during lunch breaks have occurred, often followed by stretching and prolonged yawns. Would you explain please when these behaviors first started?

Beth: Oh, I'd guess about two weeks ago.

Psychiatrist: I see. And what has changed over the last couple of weeks?

Bob: It's not easy to explain. I feel like a voice in my head is directing my actions! It's like my free will is gone!

Psychiatrist: And you, Beth?

Beth: Well, yeah! I require cat naps on a daily basis. Our doctors agree the malaise is not health related and suggested we seek your assistance.

Psychiatrist: OK, then let's use a hypnotic technique and regress to that point in time when the problem began.

N: A deep state of relaxation later, the session progressed to a question-and-answer period. After twenty minutes, the doctor ended the exercise and a refreshed Beth and Bob wanted answers.

Psychiatrist: Well first, let me assure you this is not a breakdown of any kind. I'm quite certain your mental state is quite healthy. I attribute the problem to an outside influence as yet to be determined.

Beth: That's a relief! Could we wrap this up? I believe our kitten is in need of immediate attention at home.

Psychiatrist: That's it! Your outside influence and your kitten are one and the same! You've both displayed an unusually profound concern for your cat's comfort and well-being. What would you attribute that to?

Bob: Now that you mention it, since that snowstorm two weeks ago and our subsequent housebound couple of days with Stephanie, we've been under some kind of spell! Doctor, you wouldn't believe what she's capable of.

~ *Act 3* ~

N: Minutes later, an unhappy couple of pet owners were home and in search of their cat.

Bob: There you are! We want to speak to you!

Stephy: This doesn't sound good. An attitude adjustment moment is needed here! ALRIGHT THEN! You're to follow my suggestions sent telepathically and fluff up that pillow for my nap!

Beth: Here's that catnip mousey she's been playing with. I wonder if the toy might be part of the problem?

Bob: Could be. It came into the house just before the big snowstorm. Where did you get it from?

Beth: It was a gift from the vet's office! I felt certain it would be alright for her to play with. Do you think overexposure to its contents had something to do with this mess?

Bob: I'm certain of it! I'll remove it immediately!

Stephy: Catnip mousey? No! How could this go so horribly wrong?

N: With the toy gone, her powers of concentration also left her. Trying to regain her influence over her humans proved futile, and she became depressed.

Beth: Wow, what a change has come over her! Look! She's hiding under the chair!

Bob: Looks like a case of regret! You know there should be therapy available for kittens! Maybe a referral could be arranged?

Rise of the Phoenix

Cast

N: Narrator

Stephy, Stephanie: House cat able to speak fluently to all non-human characters

Beth: Stephanie's owner, married to Bob

Bob: Stephanie's owner, married to Beth

Phoenix: Confused predatory bird

Mr. Kelly: Neighbor happy to be alive

Mrs. Kelly: Neighbor and Mr. Kelly's wife

Slither: Harmless garter snake

~Act 1~

N: Our story opens far from a little house on Bennett Street. On a hot day in August, up on a mountain in Wyoming, a volcanic cauldron was brewing. An eagle's nest with several small chicks was unfortunately situated on an overlooking ledge. Mother and chicks saw the danger and flew off, leaving behind the smallest who as yet was unable to fly. The abandoned baby had the unusual appearance of being half eagle and half peacock. Its small body is diminished further by an enormous pair of wings.

Phoenix: They're gone! I'm all alone now, and the earth is erupting all around me.

N: Super-heated steam soon enveloped the area, overwhelming the chick and putting her into a semi-conscious state of delusion. Fire from the cavernous pit forming below sent shooting sparks upward, igniting the nest and engulfing the bird. Luckily, a strong wind kicked up and sent the nest and its inhabitant miles into the air, catching the jet stream and landing half a continent away. Sadly upon landing, the chick succumbed to its injuries when suddenly…

Phoenix: Where am I? What is this place? Why am I sitting in a fire-ruined nest? Man, am I hungry!

N: The bird's rebirth was truly remarkable. She has emerged from the flames fully grown and many times her original size. She has also acquired flaming red eyes and a vocal screech loud enough to shatter glass.

Phoenix: It's almost night. Mom says the hunt's always better at night.

~*Act 2*~

N: For the next three days, the newspapers were full of stories of missing pets and damaged roofs. Neighborhood watches were in effect all over the city. Like everyone else, Beth and Bob were concerned for their pet's safety and kept Stephanie indoors at all times.

Beth: She's at it again! How many times can she possibly run from window to window?

Stephy: I'm innocent, I tell you! I don't know why I'm incarcerated, but I can provide an airtight alibi against any charge!

Bob *(reading a newspaper)*: The Kellys' cat next door is missing! This is getting way to close! Let's lock Stephy in the basement.

Stephy: Yeah? In your dreams!

N: A deafening crash brought the cat owners to their living room picture window. It seems a book end and a kitten were on the front lawn.

Phoenix *(to himself)*: Think I'll check out the playground during the day. Food's getting a little scarce around here at night.

N: With that, the great bird effortlessly lifted off his perch high atop Prospect Hill and scoured the neighborhoods from far above. His keen vision detected every movement below while his empty belly urged him onward.

Mrs. Kelly: Hey, is that Beth's cat out on our porch? Try to grab her quick before she goes missing too.

Mr. Kelly: Right! I'm sure they're trying to keep her in until the danger's over. Any word yet on our Fluffy?

Stephy: What's with everybody? They're trying to grab me too? What the heck did I do?!

~ *Act 3* ~

N: Stephanie finally found refuge under the slide at Lowell Field's playground. Shaken and confused, she was about to head home when she heard…

Slither: Where are you going? Why not stay for lunch? My lunch that issssssssssssssssss!

Stephy *(giving the snake a kick)***:** Get lost, garter snake! You're even more helpless than I am.

N: The poor snake ended up out in the open, and the bird of prey rocketed down upon him. Fortunately for Slither, hunger made the killer misjudge his descent, and the bird's razorlike talons sliced through an electrical power line instead. A brilliant burst of flame consumed the bird instantly, leaving only ashes behind.

Stephy: What the heck was that? Wait a minute, the thing's back from the dead! Run for it!

Mr. Kelly *(from his front yard)***:** Did you see that? That beast rose from the ashes bigger and stronger than before! Stephy, come here! Someone help! It's coming after me!

N: Members of the neighborhood watch were frantically dialing 911 when a scampering Stephanie inadvertently stepped on an iron pipe, flipping it high into the air and piercing the great bird of prey.

Mrs. Kelly: I saw that! Stephanie saved my husband by killing the bird!

Police *(arriving and looking down at the body)***:** Why all the fuss? There's nothing here but a tiny, weird-looking, dead baby chick. How could something like that hurt anybody?

Mr. Kelly: You're looking at a Phoenix. Legend dictates it could only be killed with an iron spear. The real question is, how did Stephy know that?

Knives and Turks and Caicos

Cast

N: Narrator

Stephy, Stephanie: House cat able to speak fluently to all non-human characters

Beth: Stephanie's owner, married to Bob

Bob: Stephanie's owner, married to Beth

Concierge: Hotel employee with an agenda

~ Act 1 ~

N: Our story opens approximately fourteen hundred miles south of a little house on Bennett Street. Hurricane season in the Caribbean was coming to an end as the month of November was drawing to a close. Beth and Bob have brought little Stephanie to the island of Grand Turk for a working vacation.

Beth: Here we are in paradise! Let's unpack and hit the beaches! Work can wait a while longer.

Bob: You've got it! What about Stephy?

Stephy: Yeah, what about Stephy? Where are my sunglasses?

N: Plans changed abruptly with a single knock on their door.

Concierge: Telegram for Elizabeth, sign here please.

Beth (*opening the envelope*)**:** They still have telegram messages here?

Bob: You look horrified! What does it say?

Beth: It's from my editor at *History Today Magazine.* He's informing me the article is due on Tuesday of next week. That's a week less than I thought I had! What are we going to do? I'm sitting here without an outline!

Bob: That still gives us six days and nights!

Stephy: Why all the fuss? Humans! One little piece of paper and they act like we're out of cat food!

Bob: A thousand ships have gone down off these reefs! I'm certain these Turks and Caicos islands won't let you down!

Beth: Sorry, those ships have all been accounted for. We need something new to accentuate something old. Like the magazine's name says, History Today.

Bob: It'll come to us. Come on, let's take a little stroll.

~Act 2~

N: Hurricane Dorian blew in during their fourth day there. No one went anywhere as the storm intensified just off the coast.

Concierge: Please don't venture out. The forecast is awfully grim.

Bob: How bad will it get?

Concierge: Landfall tonight, possibly as a category five! Waves upward of forty feet with at least ten inches of rain. Who knows what if anything will be left!

Beth: Sounds like good writing weather.

N: Stephanie could sense the approaching storm and hid under the couch. No amount of coaxing would convince her to re-emerge.

Bob: Let's ride out the storm in style. Champagne all around?

N: The following morning found the entire group combing the beach just outside the hotel. As prophesied, the devastation was tremendous.

Beth: Look at the debris the ocean has brought in!

Stephy: Look at that seagull peck at that pile of seaweed!

N: A flash and the seagull has been displaced by a curious kitten.

Bob: Stephy's found something! Look! It's an old, smashed lockbox with an antique corked bottle still intact within it.

N: Upon even closer inspection, Bob found a rolled-up parchment inside the bottle.

Bob: Hey, it's some kind of map! The Spanish inscription speaks of a dagger and the name Giacomo Columbus. The map indicates a location on this island somewhere inside an old cemetery.

Beth: Giacomo! He's Christopher Columbus's brother! Chris had another brother, Bartholomew, who was the mapmaker in the family.

Bob: Yeah? Well it says here they all ended up in jail on the island of Hispaniola for six weeks during his third voyage here before going back to Spain. Why the map describes this island is a mystery to me. And who's buried in the cemetery along with the knife?

~ *Act 3* ~

N: The trio took their findings to the concierge at the hotel's front desk. There they asked for directions to the oldest cemetery in the southernmost part of Grand Turk.

Concierge: Christopher's brother, Bartholomew, had an illegitimate daughter named Maria whose existence brought shame upon the family.

That might explain the "Maria descansa con paz" at the parchment's bottom. Translated, it would mean "Maria rest with peace." The knife pictured above it is a depiction of the Dagger Ethereal thought to perfect to exist by most historians. Should it actually exist, it would be quite the find, and to link the two would rewrite history! The baby was lost to the world!

Bob: What would the knife be worth today?

Concierge: Millions at the very least! It was fabled to belong to the Spanish Crown's lineage. Perhaps a gift to Columbus?

Beth: My article is writing itself! Let's check out the cemetery!

N: The trip took less than an hour, and upon arriving…

Bob: Wow is this place in ruins! It's so overgrown with vegetation I don't think we could ever find the grave!

Beth: The concierge mentioned the best place to look would be the furthest reaches of the graveyard. He said back then wooden crosses were used instead of stone to mark a burial site. How would he know so much about this?

Bob: Who cares? Let's explore! Where's Stephy? She was just here!

N: Stephy was twenty feet ahead chasing a butterfly when…

Beth: I hear her! Sounds like she's in pain!

N: Stephanie had leaped for the butterfly and caught her rear paw in the process.

Bob: Here! By the old tree! I'll get her down!

Beth: Yikes! Look at this inscription!

N: The wooden cross displayed a carving—a baby and a knife. The faded wording may have read "Maria Descansa Con Paz."

Bob: Help me get Stephy down. Her paw is caught in the wood!

N: Together, they extracted the kitten only to find…

Beth: The knife! Hidden inside the cross! The wood was so rotted, it fell apart around it! It's beautiful!

Concierge: I'll take that, young lady. Both of you move over to the tree! No funny business or I'll use this gun.

Bob: Where did you come from?

Concierge: We're on an island, remember? There's a boat launch just outside the cemetery grounds. That's where we're going! Start walking!

N: Just then, Stephanie jumped back up onto the cross and launched herself at the gunman. Startled, he took a step backward and fell due to the dense vegetation around his feet. Bob scooped up the revolver while Beth called the authorities with her cell phone.

Beth: The police officer I spoke to said we'd have to report the dagger's existence to the island's historical society. He sounded hopeful we'd come out financially ahead for the find. They'll take this fellow off our hands immediately upon their arrival as well.

Bob: That's great! I'll bet you'll have something for your editor too!

Stephy: Hey! Let's remember who caught the guy, OK?

Stephanie Passes the Bar

Cast

N: Narrator

Stephy, Stephanie: House cat able to speak fluently to all non-human characters

Beth: Stephanie's owner, married to Bob

Bob: Stephanie's owner, married to Beth

Tom Cat: Friend of Stephanie

Judge: Understanding authority of the court

~Act 1~

N: Your honor, our story opens in a little house on Bennett Street. Pursuant to circumstances beyond their control, my clients (Beth and Bob) plead for this court's kind indulgence and will attempt to recap the events leading to the present set of charges against one Stephanie. To this end, we will try to convince the jury this kitten, being a four-footed walking disaster, is merely prone to bouts of curiosity and subsequent trouble. Please consider the following and try not to be swayed by this the most recent episode…

Beth: Stephanie, we've got to go now! Where are you?

Stephy: If she thinks I'm going to answer and blow this great hiding place, she's nuts!

Bob: She's not in the bedroom. I'll check the kitchen.

Stephy: I'm not there either.

Beth: How does she know when it's time to see the V-E-T?

Bob: Cat radar, I think.

Beth: Ah Bob, has the coffee table grown a tail recently?

Bob: Bingo!

Stephy: Rats!

Beth: OK, Stephy, into the traveling baskets.

Bob: I'll take her down to the car, you lock up here.

Beth: OK, and I'll call ahead to confirm the appointment we made.

N: All are now safely in the car and two-thirds of the group are happy to be out in the sunshine. The remaining 33 percent, however, has other ideas.

Stephy: I'm breaking out of here! No traveling basket alive can hold me for long!

Beth: Bob, we better pull over, she's half out of the carrier now.

N: As Bob pulls the car over, Stephy jumps out!

Stephy: Free, free, I tell you!

N: It's out of the basket and through the window. The Houdini of Bennett Street strikes again!

Beth: I can't believe it, Bob! She's escaped into thin air!

Bob: Let's find her quick before she runs into trouble.

N: Ah yes, trouble, Stephanie's middle name.

Stephy: What is this place? I've never been here before. I'm getting a little nervous.

N: The scene fades with Stephanie alone in a strange place and Beth and Bob frantically searching in the wrong direction.

~Act 2~

N: Within a half hour, night has completely darkened the park Stephy has wandered into and a different breed of animal takes over.

Stephy *(ears up)***:** Who is it? Who's there?

N: The noise stops then starts again, this time moving in Stephy's direction.

Stephy: Come out of the shadows or you're lunch, fella!

N: Emerging into the light appears a ragged-looking older cat who could do with a meal and a bath.

Tom Cat: You talking to me?

Stephy *(braver than she feels)*: Yeah! What's the idea of scaring me half to death?

Tom Cat: I don't think I've seen you here before, are you lost?

N: The two become friends and soon Tom Cat is helping Stephy adjust to a very different way of life.

Tom Cat: You see, in this neighborhood, you steal first and eat later. You must be hungry. I know I am! Let's go!

N: Stephy quickly finds there is competition for what little food there is out there.

Tom Cat: Stephy, stop! Look around. This is the gang's area. Don't touch anything. Just run this way NOW!

N: Stephy and Tom Cat run like the wind, which is good because there were many breezes right behind them!

Stephy *(out of breath)*: Got to stop! (Huff puff) Can't go on!

Tom Cat: OK, I think we're safe now! It's clear you weren't cut out for this. Where are you from?

N: Stephy explains about life on Bennett Street to her amazed new friend. She also finds their worlds are about as different as night and day.

Tom Cat: I thought you were a rich cat! Look, Stephy, I don't know how you got here, but I'm going to get you back!

~ *Act 3* ~

N: Our two drifters are on the move again. First they make the trash can rounds, then it's back to the streets to find Beth and Bob. All the while, their travels take them toward another tough area: the river.

Stephy: What is this ocean we've come to? Looks like someone pulled the plug and all the waters rushing down the drain!

Tom Cat *(laughing)*: Oh, Stephy, this is the river! The current makes the water move, no drain here. Come on, I have friends who might have seen Beth and Bob.

N: A few more yards and the night is suddenly split by the glare of a large campfire. Shadowy figures moving back and forth make the whole scene seem rather unreal.

Stephy: What is this place?

Tom Cat: It's the river town! Come on, I'll show you around!

N: Introductions and inquiries bring almost immediate results. Someone had indeed seen Beth and Bob just twenty minutes ago back at the park.

Tom Cat: Thanks guys! Let's get back there quick, Stephy!

N: Meanwhile, Beth and Bob are about to give up! With no sign of Stephy and night settling in, there's nothing else to do but go home!

Beth: What could've happened? It's like this place just swallowed her up!

Bob: Ugh! What a way to go! Let's give it another few minutes.

N: Meanwhile, the cat gang is also closing in. They're on the fringe of the park over by the bar.

Stephy: Hey, I see Beth and Bob! Come on, let's go!

Tom Cat: Hold on, Stephy! Look over at the bar! That's the worst cat gang in the city, and we can't get to the park without passing them!

Stephy: So what?

Tom Cat: Are you crazy? That's the group that chased us earlier. I'm telling you, they're killers.

Stephy: OK, Tom Cat, I understand. Look, it's been great meeting you, and I really appreciate the help you've given me.

Tom Cat: You mean you're going anyway?

Stephy: Yep!

Tom Cat: OK, but not alone! Look, we'll do it this way…

N: After a hushed huddle, the two suddenly take to the high road!

Stephy: Tom Cat, I can't do this!

Tom Cat: Sure you can! Look, just step off the roof like this and on to the telephone wire.

N: A few tentative steps and they're halfway across the street.

Stephy: OOOOH! The wind! I'm going to fall!

Tom Cat: Now that's the dumbest idea I've ever heard!

N: A glance over his shoulder proves most informative. Two cat gang members are on the roof with wire cutters!

Tom Cat: Stephy, don't look down! Just do as I do!

N: Tom cat pulls the wire up to his tummy and does a fast-forward crawl. With more cat gang members in the street just below, it doesn't look good!

Beth: What is that terrible noise?

Bob: Sounds like a cat fight! Hurry!

N: Just as Beth and Bob arrive, our high wire act takes a plunge.

Stephy: We're falling! Help!

N: Who said it's raining cats and dogs?

Bob: Beth, catch Stephy, I'll catch the other one!

N: Stephy falls into Beth's arms while the cat gang scatters! Unfortunately, the police also arrive due to neighborhood complaints and take everyone downtown!

Judge: Alright, I've heard enough! I can see this malicious mischief was the work of the cat gang and not Tom Cat and Stephanie. You are all free to go!

N: Oh happy day! Stephy, Bob, and Beth head for home. Tom Cat is given a new home and job as the official courthouse cat. And the police are out picking up the cat gang! Be sure you're here next time when Stephy gets over this and starts out again to change the world.

Stephanie's Secret

Cast

N: Narrator

Stephy, Stephanie: House cat able to speak fluently to all non-human characters

Beth: Stephanie's owner, married to Bob

Bob: Stephanie's owner, married to Beth

Big Guy: Stephanie's brother

Hey You: Stephanie's mother

~*Act 1*~

N:　　Our story begins in a little house on Bennett Street. Early spring has brought an explosion of life as Stephanie soon discovers during her morning routine of window-hopping.

Stephy:　Wow! What's going on out there? I'm certain there was nothing but snow in the backyard yesterday. Now there's nothing but green out there today? I wonder if the folks know about this.

N:　　Stephanie creeps into the bedroom and launches herself through the air, landing on a sleeping Bob's face.

Stephy *(to herself)*: Wake up, get up, the sun's up, you know. Boy, I like starting the day this way!

Bob:　What's this? Are you kidding me? Stephy, you better hide well for the next month or two!

N:　　Her job done, Stephanie runs full tilt toward the door as her fantastic ears pick up a faint noise outside.

Stephy:　The great beyond calls. I'll see you guys later. Oh, what's this?

N:　　Moments later, an outdoor crash has everyone up and looking out the front room window. Before morning coffee, the drama isn't appreciated.

Stephy *(to herself)*: Hey, did you hear that? Invasionary forces are at work here! Check the doors and windows! Remember, I'm right behind you!

N:　　The perpetrator was gone in a flash, but the damage was everywhere.

Bob:　It's alright, Beth, just a squirrel or something knocking over the birdbath in the front yard. How about a breakfast break?

Beth:　Sounds good. Stephanie has an empty bowl too.

N: The group sits down to a peaceful meal when suddenly another catastrophe occurred. The backyard window box and lattice came crashing down accompanied by an unearthly yowl.

Bob: You finish up here, Beth. I'll see what's going on out there.

N: This time Bob catches a glimpse of a tail as he enters the yard and runs after what he thinks is a raccoon. He then quickly loses sight of the beast as it dives into a pile of firewood.

Beth *(from the window)*: Are you alright? What was it?

Bob: Yeah, I'm fine but no, I haven't a clue what that thing was! Keep Stephy inside. That phantom was no lightweight!

~ Act 2 ~

N: The wary group, now inside, tries to make sense of the whole episode. Without a good look at the animal, they're at a loss as to how to proceed. Finally Beth decides it's time to call for help.

Bob *(at the door)*: Hi, animal control, please come right in.

N: An intense dialogue ensues and traps are promptly placed around the property.

Beth: Are we sure those cages won't harm whatever's out there?

Bob: No, he said they only contain the animals for future release in the wild.

N: Once again, a noise so faint the humans can't hear is picked up by Stephanie. This time the basement is the place to be, and without thinking, Stephanie runs down the stairs.

Big Guy: Hey, over here! You've got to help me!

Stephy: Where are you?

Big Guy: Behind the furnace, over by the water heater.

Stephy: OK, but step out into the light.

N: Big Guy does and Stephanie is treated to an exact likeness of herself, only much bigger.

Stephy: Who are you? Why are you here? You look more like me than I do!

Big Guy: They call me Big Guy. I'm your long-lost brother.

Stephy: How did you find me? Where have you been?

Big Guy: I visited Mom by the store and she told me where to find you.

Stephy: Right! I've been there too. But where have you been all this time?

Big Guy: Remember when we were both in the box with Mom? Something happened while you two slept.

Stephy: What?

Big Guy: Well, you won't believe this, but I got carried out by strangers and put in a car. When they finally stopped, I was able to escape. I've been on the run ever since!

Stephy: You dunderhead. They were trying to take you home.

Big Guy: I WAS HOME!

Stephy: I mean they were trying to make you part of their family.

N: The two talked about old times, or at least what they could remember of their brief past together. Stephanie suggests Big Guy stay with her, but he won't hear of it. Sometimes it's all for the best.

~ *Act 3* ~

N: Feeding time is a long way off, and Stephanie has little to offer before Big Guy's inevitable departure. Still curious though, she stalls for time by asking question after question hoping to change his mind.

Stephy: How did you get your name?

Big Guy: Are you kidding? Look at me!

Stephy: OK, how much do you weigh?

Big Guy: Twenty-eight pounds and you?

Stephy: Six pounds at the last vet visit.

Big Guy: Sorry, sis, I've got to go. Let's meet at Mom's sometime?

N: Just then, Beth comes down the stairs on her way to the laundry center. She is about to greet Stephanie when she sees a large figure shoot past her.

Beth: Ahhhh! What was that thing?

Stephy (*to herself*): That thing was my brother, and I'm out of here too!

Beth: Bob, come quick, Stephy's escaped!

N: Moments later, Bob arrives and is informed Stephanie is out chasing a gorilla.

Bob: Are you sure? It's pretty dark down here.

Beth: I'm telling you, it was huge and furry, and Stephy's out chasing it now!

N: The two cat owners search the neighborhood without success. Not knowing what else to do, they post signs offering a reward for her safe return. Meanwhile several blocks away…

Stephy: Hold up, Big Guy, I have something for you.

Big Guy: Stephy, I'm in a hurry. There's something I've got to do.

Stephy: Well at least look behind you. There's someone with me.

N: Big Guy does stop and as he turns, we hear…

Hey You: Son! Your sister and I want to give you a decent send-off.

Big Guy: Mom, where did you come from?

Hey You: I'm never far away, just call when you need me.

Big Guy: Wow, family when I need it! I'd forgotten what that's like. My travels have changed me. I'm not who you remember. The laws of the jungle have made me a killer. It's how I feed myself.

N: With that, he was gone.

Stephy: What do you think? Will he ever be back?

Hey You: I think he belongs to the world now. Be happy for what we had.

BATH
DISHES
BLANKE

The Blanket Sequence

Cast

N: Narrator

Stephy, Stephanie: House cat able to speak fluently to all non-human characters

Beth: Stephanie's owner, married to Bob

Bob: Stephanie's owner, married to Beth

Russet: Friend of Stephanie

Police: Ordinary officers

~*Act 1*~

N: Our story opens in a little house on Bennett Street. Spring has finally arrived, bringing life back to the area with warm breezes outside and open windows inside. On just such a day, Stephanie is strolling through the living room when…

Stephy: Ah, what have we here? Boxes in the living room? How kind of them to provide extra sleeping accommodations for me.

N: Upon closer inspection, she finds a luxurious added bonus.

Stephy: Soft clothing! Inside the boxes! What a country!

N: No sooner has she leaped into the nearest box when Beth enters the room and spoils the moment.

Beth: Out! I just cleaned those things! What's wrong with you?

Stephy *(in a huff)***:** Humans, you try to bring them up right, and look what happens.

N: Beth takes the box to the next room while Stephanie jumps into box number two.

Stephy: Oh, blankets in this one! I'll pull the box cover over to ensure privacy. No need to go through that irritation twice.

N: Not the best move, Stephanie. Beth again enters and snaps the box lid in place before taking it to the next room as well.

Bob: Keep them coming, Beth. I'll bring the car around and load up. There's plenty of space in storage, we may even have time for more.

Stephy: What? Get me out of here! Why me?

N: Thankfully the box has ventilation slots built in. Unfortunately Stephanie's cries are muffled by the blankets she is hiding under. Some days are better than others.

~Act 2~

N: Bob loads several more cartons into the minivan and carts them off to the storage facility. The unit itself is a brightly lit clean caged affair with space enough for all their off-season clothing. Luckily, Stephanie's box is placed on top of the others.

Stephy: Well alright, the world has stopped shaking! I'm hearing a door banging, and since when have we left lights on in the basement? Hey, no biggie, I'll just pop the lid and go back up to the den.

Russet: Hey, you in the box! Come out here slowly with your paws up!

Stephy *(to herself)*: I don't think I'm in the basement anymore.

N: Slowly she pops the lid and, squinting against the bright lights, she climbs down to confront the silhouetted figure.

Stephy: A raccoon? You nearly scared me to death! I've had a bad day, you know. So what's your story and where are we anyway?

Russet: We're in a warehouse of some kind. I've checked, there's no way out. The good news is I've found food and water! How did you end up here?

N: Stephanie explains in detail how she was abducted and left for dead. Then it occurs to her…

Stephy: There maybe is a way out yet! Why don't we make a break for it when the next human arrives?

Russet: And when might that be?

Stephy: Oh right, I guess we won't know until it happens. How long have you been here?

Russet: Long enough to know that when the food runs out, we're done!

Stephy: Alright, let's have a look around. Maybe we'll think of something.

~ *Act 3* ~

N: Things back on Bennett Street also start to unravel as the seasonal change brings more questions than answers.

Beth: Did we pack away all the sweaters in the hall closet? I meant to save a few here for the cooler days.

Bob: I can't recall packing them. I'll check the closet. Nope, none left in here. I did find Stephy's toy ball though. Have you seen her around?

Beth: Not since I shooed her away from the boxes. Strange though, she usually wants dinner about now.

N: A through-search of the house later...

Beth: She must have got out somehow. Should we check the neighborhood?

Bob: No, let's rest up. I'm sure she'll be scratching at the door soon.

N: The "rest-up" time was elongated due to an unexpected nap. Upon awaking, both are famished and go out to a restaurant for dinner. Back at the storage unit, Stephy and Russet are tired and hungry as well.

Stephy: I'm starved! What did you find to eat?

Russet: Dog food! A big bag of it! Why the face? Don't you want some?

Stephy: I think I'll pass. Hey, did you hear that? Someone's outside!

Russet: Yeah, it's past closing time though. Maybe it's the owner.

Stephy: Who cares? It's our ticket out of here! Get ready to rush the door.

N: Suddenly Stephanie hears the soft sounds of a pick in a lock.

Stephy: We might want to hold off on that rush-the-door idea.

Russet: Yeah, I heard it too. What should we do?

Stephy: Attack the feet! I'll take the left, you take the other left!

N: The door silently slides open, and a figure moves into the room. The bright lights temporarily blind the intruder, and the attacking animals make him fall backward onto the security panel. A silent alarm is then sent to police headquarters.

Stephy: Russet, let's book it out of here before he gets to his sore feet!

Russet: Can't do it! He fell against the door and closed it tight! We're trapped in here with a wounded maniac!

N: Stephy jumps up to her original box, knocking it over onto the intruder and covering him in blankets. Again unable to see, the would-be thief steps forward and lands on Russet's tail. The raccoon's howl is deafening.

Police Officers *(arriving with guns drawn)*: Hold it right there!

Russet: Door's open, Stephy, I'm out of here!

N: The police, the intruder, and Stephanie proceed to the police station where thanks to the phone number on her collar, Beth receives a text message to pick her up.

Beth: Oh, Bob, care to take a little car ride?